**Evan intended to find the truth—
and the killer—one way or another**

Rowen was next on the madman's kill list and Evan understood what the message he'd left behind meant. He didn't like bringing Rowen along, but he couldn't, especially now, risk letting her out of his sight for even one second.

Six people were dead and the one and only clue any of the murders yielded was the tattoo found on the victims.

The rain had started to fall once more. A storm had descended, bringing with it wrathful and ominous thunder along with the accompanying jagged bolts of vengeful lightning. Dark amassed in the sky, providing relief from the sun for him, but giving Boston the dismal look of a city grieving for its loss. The city looked murky, depressed...and eerily crying out for justice.

A city under siege by unknown sinister forces.

Dear Harlequin Intrigue Reader,

Summer's winding down, but Harlequin Intrigue is as hot as ever with six spine-tingling reads for you this month!

* Our new BIG SKY BOUNTY HUNTERS promotion debuts with Amanda Stevens's *Going to Extremes*. In the coming months, look for more titles from Jessica Andersen, Cassie Miles and Julie Miller.

* We have some great miniseries for you. Rita Herron is back with *Mysterious Circumstances,* the latest in her NIGHTHAWK ISLAND series. Mallory Kane's *Seeking Asylum* is the third book in her ULTIMATE AGENTS series. And Sylvie Kurtz has another tale in THE SEEKERS series—*Eye of a Hunter.*

* No month would be complete without a chilling gothic romance. This month's ECLIPSE title is Debra Webb's *Urban Sensation.*

* Jan Hambright, a fabulous new author, makes her debut with *Relentless.* Sparks fly when a feisty repo agent repossesses a BMW with an ex-homicide detective in the trunk!

Don't miss a single book this month and every month!

Sincerely,

Denise O'Sullivan
Senior Editor
Harlequin Intrigue

URBAN SENSATION
DEBRA WEBB

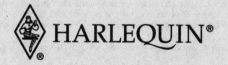

HARLEQUIN®

TORONTO • NEW YORK • LONDON
AMSTERDAM • PARIS • SYDNEY • HAMBURG
STOCKHOLM • ATHENS • TOKYO • MILAN • MADRID
PRAGUE • WARSAW • BUDAPEST • AUCKLAND

ISBN 0-373-22864-3

URBAN SENSATION

Copyright © 2005 by Debra Webb

ABOUT THE AUTHOR

Debra Webb was born in Scottsboro, Alabama, to parents who taught her that anything is possible if you want it badly enough. When her husband joined the military, they moved to Berlin, Germany, and Debra became a secretary in the commanding general's office. By 1985 they were back in the States, and with the support of her husband and two beautiful daughters, Debra took up writing full-time and in 1998 her dream of writing for Harlequin came true. You can write to Debra with your comments at P.O. Box 64, Huntland, Tennessee 37345 or visit her Web site at www.debrawebb.com to find out exciting news about her next book.

Books by Debra Webb

CAST OF CHARACTERS

Rowen O'Connor—Boston homicide detective. Rowen O'Connor has six dead bodies, all drained of their blood, and not a single clue as to a perpetrator—at least not a human one. The last thing she needs in her life right now is the man who broke her heart.

Evan Hunter—Former FBI agent. Evan Hunter went into seclusion three years ago after an explosion almost killed him. But this dark, brooding man is not the same one Rowen once knew.

Bernard Cost—Medical Examiner. Dr. Cost hasn't been able to help Rowen's case. Maybe he isn't looking closely enough.

Bart Koppel—Chief of Homicide. Koppel just wants this case solved but he wants Rowen to keep quiet about the "V" word. He appears more concerned with the politics of the case than with finding the killer.

Viktor Azariel—Self-proclaimed vampire who lives in a fifteenth-century castle he had moved all the way from England. He is connected to at least two of the victims.

Merv Gant—Rowen's partner. She trusts him with her life, but she can't tell him her secrets.

Lenny Doherty—Boston homicide detective. Rowen's team got Doherty by default. He seems reliable enough, if not overly ambitious.

Jeff Finch—Boston homicide detective. The new guy. Rowen isn't sure she trusts Finch. He's an unknown variable.

Gateway—A shadow operation under the FBI's umbrella that investigates so-called psychic phenomena. Most of the original members are retired or dead... except for one who is unaccounted for.... He could be anyone, anywhere.

Prologue

Vibrations shattered through his brain. Pain followed in their path, exploding in the very cells of gray matter, inhibiting his ability to concentrate on anything but the horrendous agony.

Evan Hunter felt his way through the darkness until he reached the door. The misery writhed inside him… building with each step he took. He prayed for death, even when he knew it would not come. Too easy, he'd decided long ago.

Whatever his sins, God had apparently concluded that he deserved this ceaseless torture.

Not even sleep provided relief anymore.

Only silence…only distance. And the mind-numbing drugs his doctor had prescribed, which he now refused to take.

Nausea roiled, leaving a bitter taste in his mouth as a second onslaught of tremors in the air set off its usual chain reaction of physical suffering. His entire body seized, shuddered with the intensity before he wrested back some semblance of control.

He jerked open the door and blinked against the invading glare of the night. He grunted at the burn searing his retinas before he squeezed his eyes shut. Where were his shades? He'd forgotten about the full moon. Forgotten about the clear night sky and all its punishingly bright stars.

"Mr. Hunter?" a voice whispered.

Evan resisted the instinctive urge to open his eyes again—couldn't handle any more exposure just now. No need to look. He would have recognized the voice and the scent of his visitor even if he hadn't gotten that fleeting glimpse of his silhouette in the moonlight before closing his eyes.

"I...I have your supplies, sir," the man croaked.

Evan didn't speak, just stepped back for Marty Kenzie to scurry inside far enough to leave the two bags of supplies on a table a mere four steps from the door.

"Payment is there," Evan told him, his voice low, guttural from the pain, as he groped in his pocket for his protective eyewear. The sound of skin rasping along cotton fabric echoed harshly against his eardrums. His fingers curled around the shades, dragged them from his pocket and slid them onto his face. With that barrier in place, he risked opening his eyes once more.

His hand shaking with trepidation, young Marty Kenzie picked up the envelope containing the money for the food, as well as payment for services rendered. That same uneasiness incited his heart to pound so hard in his thin chest that Evan worried for the boy's well-being. When he had shoved the envelope into his pocket, Marty worked up the courage to turn around, to allow his anxious gaze to settle on his employer.

"Thank you, sir," he murmured.

Evan said nothing to that.

Marty crossed the four steps back to the door as swiftly as he dared, careful to keep his gaze on that single, narrow route of escape. He was afraid of Evan…of who and what he was. But he kept coming back because Evan paid him more than anyone else had or would.

"Marty."

The young man stalled in the doorway. His posture screamed of just how badly he wanted to keep going…to flee for his life. The terror that had been mounting since he'd stepped up onto the rustic porch made his limbs tremble.

"Yes, sir?" Marty offered quietly without turning around.

"Next time, only knock once."

Marty nodded, then rushed away, careful not to step too heavily…cautiously avoiding the boards he knew from experience squeaked beneath his underweight frame. He flung himself into the old car he hoped to be able to replace once he finished his masters and started his career in architecture. He remembered in the nick of time not to slam the car door. Sweat had by now risen on his skin, forming a film that heightened the anxiety already radiating through him.

Evan closed and bolted the door, blocking out the world, before his courier could start the engine of his vehicle or turn on the headlights.

Impatient to satisfy the questions haunting his every thought, conscious as well as unconscious, he moved to the side table and fished through the bags, his hands rustling loudly against brown paper until he found what he wanted.

Evan took the *Boston Reporter* Marty Kenzie had found at one of the large chain bookstores in Richmond and relocated to the chair where he spent most of his unstructured time. Magazines and newspapers lay in organized stacks around his reading area. All delivered by Marty or his predecessor. Here, this deep in the mountains, there was no home delivery of newspapers or even any mail. No telephone. Wouldn't have been any electricity had Evan not invested a small fortune in the local utilities company for installation of the service. The cost was of no consequence. He had little use for his money now.

He sat down and clicked on the reading lamp occupying a prominent position on the table near his chair. The lamp was adjustable and equipped with a special nonglare, low-wattage bulb. Its twin resided on a similar table next to his bed. There were no other lights in the house.

He unfolded the paper, anticipation making his hands

tremble the way Marty's had moments ago, as he read the headlines his dreams had already forecast.

Vampires In Boston. Third Victim Discovered. Police Baffled.

Evan read on, his jaw set against the anger brewing deep in his gut. When his eyes found her name in bold black print, fury roared through him, tripping that internal alarm that warned of the misery that would follow. But he didn't care. She was in danger. He had sensed as much for weeks, had dreamed of her fate more than once.

Now he had proof that his concerns were not just nightmares brought on by dwelling in the past. The danger was real. It was happening *now.*

There was only one way to alter her fate.

Risk his own.

Chapter One

As luck would have it, the abysmal rain had finally stopped. Only about four or five hours too late to save the situation that was likely unsalvageable from the moment another young life had ended in Detective Rowen O'Connor's jurisdiction.

The proverbial ethnic cocktail of dozens of nationalities, Boston's South End sprawled adjacent to and south of Back Bay. Three- and four-story stooped red-brick row houses dotted the short streets running perpendicular to the main thoroughfares. What had once been tired lodging houses in a shabby backwater neighborhood separated by railroad tracks from the more desirable northern half of Boston had slowly been reclaimed and revitalized by cunning developers with visions of grandeur.

Progress, however well-intentioned and welcome, had not saved the life of Carlotta Simpson.

The crush of darkness and the urgency of time in combination with the elements had forced Boston PD to set up low-heat floodlights around the body, lighting the gruesome details for all to see. The young woman lay facedown in an awkward death sprawl. She wore the black slacks and tee that sported the logo of the Southie pub where she had waitressed five nights per week during the past eighteen months. The sixty bucks she'd earned in tips on last night's shift were still in her purse, along with her driver's license, a Filene's Basement credit card and various other feminine accessories such as lip gloss, mints and a hairbrush.

Homicide Detective Rowen O'Connor stared up at the buildings on either side of the alley where the victim's body lay and considered how sad it was that she'd been so very close to safety and yet so far away. Only yards from the place she'd called home for two years.

The buildings on this block had yet to be renovated in the latest rebirth efforts. Most were badly in need of too many repairs to list and gave off a sense of aging gloom that would only worsen as dawn approached.

Not exactly the breeding ground for young aspirations.

Rowen had already concluded what kind of dreams the victim had clung to when she closed her eyes at night and no longer saw the dilapidated walls surrounding her. No longer dwelled on the blisters her shoes had rubbed on her feet as she worked an extra shift at the pub, which, according to her employer, she did quite often.

The posters of the glamorous women she admired, all well-known supermodels, and stacks of fashion magazines had offered a big clue as to the secret fantasies

Carlotta Simpson had sheltered behind soft brown eyes and long, brunette hair. The perfect white teeth now bared by the scowl of horror frozen on her face, the above-average height and slender size four body she had daydreamed would get her noticed and help her to break into that exciting field someday no longer mattered.

She was dead.

A next of kin hadn't been located as yet. Her neighbors barely knew her. When not working, she attended undergraduate classes at Wellesley College and was rarely at home for much other than to sleep or change clothes. According to her employer, who seemed to know her better than anyone they'd interviewed thus far, the victim had been a good student…a nice girl in every sense of the word.

Nothing Rowen had learned offered the first clue as to why the woman might have been murdered. She had no known enemies and, from all reports, was not involved in any high-risk activities.

A woman who'd claimed to be suffering from insomnia, as well as morning sickness related to her pregnancy, had stuck her head out her bathroom window for some fresh air and saw what she perceived to be a body. She'd called 911 and the rest was documented history.

The boys in blue had assessed the dead woman's condition, noted the similarity of her unusual injury to those in three previous murders, secured the scene and called in the homicide detective on duty. That detective, in turn, had called Rowen since she was lead investigator on the homicide case with similar victims stacking up like a cord of wood.

Rowen scanned the windows as she walked along the alley. Some lit, most dark. It was quite early, but the time wouldn't have mattered. Urban tenants learned from the get-go that when the red and blue lights pulsed in their neighborhood, questions usually followed. So they turned out their lamps and pretended not to notice that something vile had visited their community. But that hadn't stopped the uniforms from beating on doors. Between those interviews and what Rowen had gleaned from the victim's employer, she had a pretty good start, considering she'd been on the scene for one hour and forty-five minutes. That small cluster of information was only the beginning for what they needed to get the job done.

With four cruisers and the medical examiner's van fanned out as an additional layer of security against intrusion, passage on this Roxbury end of Massachusetts Avenue had been narrowed to one lane. The reporters who'd arrived hadn't helped. At least two news vans had made it to the scene before Rowen. Soon the first of morning rush hour traffic would funnel into the cool October morning and the blockage would soon escalate into a serious traffic problem. One that would earn Boston PD more bad press in the media, as well as numerous complaints called into the mayor's office. Bostonians did not like being put out…not even for murder.

Admittedly, this city was much more suited to walking or bicycling or use of the T, the public transit system. Driving could prove trying, if not downright nerve-racking, considering the downtown streets still followed the path of their forerunners—cattle trails. Traffic was hell and most drivers were impatient, Rowen included.

But walking at night, especially late at night, was not a good idea in certain areas.

Carlotta Simpson had learned that lesson the hard way.

In the victim's apartment, designated as a part of the secondary crime scene, there were no signs of forced entry and all appeared to be in order. The pub where she worked would also fall under that umbrella. Those two locations were the last places the victim had been seen alive before ending up dead in this depressing alley.

After a sweep by the crime scene techs, the apartment had been sealed until someone who knew Carlotta could be located. An individual or individuals who had been in her apartment fairly often would more likely notice if anything were missing or out of place. Otherwise, there wasn't much chance Rowen would glean anything from the victim's personal belongings other than what she already had. She could hope that some note or phone number found in the apartment or a description of a patron the victim had encountered at her workplace would lead to whoever had killed her, but the chances weren't that good.

Police tape hung on either end of the alley, marking

the area as the official primary crime scene and serving as a second level of deterrence for curious onlookers, including the press corps gathering force with each passing minute.

Blasts of white light exploded over and over from a camera's flash, disrupting the darkness that reigned over the alleyway beyond the well-lit vicinity where the body remained waiting for the next leg of its final journey. The vivid slashes of light reminded Rowen of the lightning the storm had displayed earlier that evening when she'd still been at home in bed and trying to sleep. She watched for a moment as the techs worked quickly to process and document every aspect of the scene before turning it over to the medical examiner.

The M.E., Dr. Bernard Cost, a man of about sixty who had been summoned from bed at half past four in the morning, hovered close by, waiting to assume control of the body. Rowen hadn't talked to him just yet. She didn't want to color his perspective by discussing what she had concluded after one glance at the victim.

This case in particular required unshakable objectivity.

Rowen blinked to clear the spots the camera flashes had caused from her vision and resumed her search of the scene. Using her police-issue flashlight, she covered the entire length of the alley once more, moving the light from side to side, carefully scanning for blood or any damned thing else that might be related to the murder. She'd performed this walk-through examination twice already, once before the techs were allowed on site.

As lead investigator, it was her job to get a feel for the scene and organize an approach for collecting evidence. She'd had to look at the big picture and determine how best to conduct the necessary business that would facilitate speedy justice for the victim. Then there had been a second sweep with the aid of the floodlights, and now, one last painstaking scrutiny just to be sure she hadn't missed anything while hyped with the adrenaline of discovery.

She clenched her jaw and restrained the anger ramming against the wall of detachment she'd erected from the moment she received the call.

This one was just like the last one.

And the two before that.

No evidence. Not a single footprint or cigarette butt or drop of blood. No shell casing, no murder weapon. No witnesses. Nothing. The M.E. would have no better luck when he processed the body. Whoever had done this knew how to cover his tracks. There wouldn't even be the first latent print or indication of trauma. Not one damned thing.

It was as if the perp first hypnotized his victims and then sucked 'em dry.

Rowen shuddered inwardly and evicted the concept from her brain. She would not let the press hoopla color her thinking.

When Dr. Cost moved into position near the body, Rowen set aside the infuriating reality of what this fourth murder meant and headed back in that direction.

She had to do this right. No matter that she wanted to scream in frustration. How could this keep happening?

"Morning, Doc," she said, infusing her tone with a calm she in no way felt and wishing she had a cup of coffee…anything containing caffeine. She'd left the house without taking the time to brew a pot. The urgency she'd experienced upon arriving at the crime scene had morphed into anger and now into a disheartening blend of frustration and defeat.

She dropped into a crouch a few feet away from the M.E., allowing him plenty of elbow room. Though the crime scene was Rowen's domain, the M.E. had legal authority over the body. Since he was the expert, Rowen had no problem whatsoever with those boundaries. She liked boundaries. They kept her out of trouble.

Cost grunted his usual greeting. Once he dove into his initial assessment, he paid little heed to anything or anyone else around him. He palpated the deceased woman's scalp, then the neck, and downward, checking for broken bones or other readily assessable evidence of trauma. He tested the right arm.

"No rig in the larger muscles yet," he commented for Rowen's benefit.

Though the smaller muscles of her face were already affected, indicating at least a couple hours since death, the lack of rigor mortis in the muscles of the arms signified the victim had not been dead for much longer than three or four hours, tops. As Rowen watched, the doc removed a syringe from his kit and withdrew vitreous fluid from the victim's eyeball. Rowen swallowed back the bitter taste that rose in her throat but refused to look away. She needed to see all of this, to mentally document every step.

The fluid removed would provide postmortem potassium levels, which would convey an additional estimate of time of death. Core body temperature would be checked at the morgue, Rowen presumed, where the doctor could take a closer look before inserting the thermometer. Even with the floodlights, this alley was no place to look for signs of sexual assault. Removing clothing or inserting thermometers could eliminate or contaminate evidence. Dr. Cost opted not to take the risk.

The M.E. glanced at Rowen's gloved hands. "Help me turn her over." A trace sheet had already been laid in place for wrapping the body.

Rowen obliged, subconsciously registering the non-human coolness of the woman's skin. A layer of latex on her hands and paper covers on her shoes were automatics for Rowen. She never took chances with her crime scenes. Though they offered little in the way of armor shielding against the horror of death.

She'd always harbored extreme fear when it came to dying, significantly more than what most people considered normal. The panic she felt at times bordered on outright phobia. Those who knew her struggle—they were few, only her closest friends and family—couldn't understand her need to go into homicide. Rowen deemed it her little way of doing all she could to stop those who committed the worst of crimes against others. And maybe to prove she could not only face the inevitable but could wage a sort of battle against it.

Cost shook his head slowly, a heavy sigh splintering his quiet ruminations as he considered the victim. "Nothing. I see nothing, Detective, that is going to separate this victim from the others."

Rowen's apprehension amped up another notch as she watched him bag the vic's hands. "But you can't be certain just yet." She needed to hear something different but she knew that wasn't going to happen.

"Look at her, Rowen." He gestured to the grayish white skin that was strangely lacking in the usual lividity or marbling effect caused by blood pooling in the veins. "And if that isn't enough, there is no outward indication of trauma other than this." He pointed to the small marks on the victim's throat, in the area of the body's most prominent blood-carrying vessel.

"The same as the other three," he stated unnecessarily and gave a small shrug. "I'll do all I can. But I can't find evidence if it isn't there. At this point, I would say the victim died of extreme blood loss. End of story. Just like the others." He looked over at Rowen then; his entire visage grim. "The only question is, how?"

And there it was. The riddle for which she had no solution. The one thing she and Cost knew for certain was that, in the other three murders and most likely in this one, the vast majority of the victim's blood had been drained in a manner similar to how one siphons fuel from a gas tank with a hose. Only, they didn't have a hose. They had no murder weapon whatsoever.

Maybe the *Reporter* was right.

Maybe Boston had itself a vampire.

A thirsty one at that.

WHEN THE BODY had been taken away and the crime scene secured for a second evidence sweep in the light of day, Rowen peeled off the latex gloves and shoe covers and shoved them into the pocket of her blazer. A fog had lifted and the dawn had come, swathed in a chilling, morose gray that had more to do with her mood than it did with the climate.

She climbed into her car and headed to One Schroeder Plaza, the main headquarters of Boston's police department. There was time to check her messages and make some calls before the preliminary report from the autopsy would be ready. This case had priority status. Any new victims would be pushed to the front of the line. The powers that be were waiting, holding their collective breaths, for some sort of verdict. For any indication of a reasonable explanation that didn't include sidebars to the *Reporter*'s melodramatic suggestions. Just what the city needed this close to Halloween.

So far, the murders had all taken place in one area and had since become known as the South End Murders. Not exactly original, but better than some others suggested at the station. It was bad enough that a smart-ass reporter had tossed out the idea of vampires to the general public. Having anyone in Homicide mention it, even as a joke, was not good at all. Especially since the reporter couldn't have made the obvious connection if someone hadn't leaked the cause of death.

Daylight crept over the city, the sun bleaching some of the gray, as Rowen reached Columbus Avenue. But she still felt shrouded in darkness, gripped in the choke hold of uncertainty.

Though she ignored the haunting feeling when working a case, the moment she was alone, her mind no longer focused on the scene or on a related report, she felt it...stronger than ever. It was more than the sensation of being watched. Far more intimate, somehow. As if her own shadow was in a peculiar manner "following" her.

Rowen shuddered and kicked the disturbing concept out of her head.

She had bigger problems to worry about.

"Damn."

She cringed, felt like smacking her forehead with the heel of her hand. She'd left home in such a hurry this morning she couldn't remember if she'd put out any Kibbles for Princess. Definitely hadn't taken her out for a potty walk. Coming home to a puddle or worse was not among her favorite things to do. And letting the animal go all day, and possibly part of the night if an emergency came up, without food was unconscionable.

Thinking of her spoiled and pampered Maltese made Rowen smile no matter how irritating the domineering animal could be. She'd had the arrogant little piece of white fluff for two years, having rescued the dog after its original owner had been murdered and no one else had wanted a pet. Especially one who wore a genuine rhinestone collar and sported pink toenails.

The elderly woman's body hadn't been found for two days and Princess had stayed right beside her master the entire time, not leaving her side to drink or eat even though both bowls had been full and waiting. Now that was loyalty. Everyone should have someone or thing that cared that much. She supposed that was how she ended up taking the prissy pooch home. Rowen was tired of being alone.

According to the dog's registration papers and the veterinarian who'd provided her health care, she was almost five years old now.

Rowen loved her like a child.

Her smile faltered. Memories she'd thought she had laid to rest three years ago filtered into her mind as if she'd flipped that switch with the mere mention of children. She forced the thoughts away, refused to loiter in that part of her past.

There was plenty of time for finding the right life partner and starting a family. It wasn't as if thirty-one was that old. But on mornings like this one, she felt a hundred.

After parking she made her way along the slender cobblestone byway to the eighteenth-century row house she called home. Rowen had inherited the brownstone, once the home to servants of the wealthier Beacon Hill residents, from her grandmother, who was purported to have been a direct descendant of one of those servants. Rowen's family was immensely proud of its heritage, however lacking it was in the historically privileged blue blood of the area. Her mother would say, "Who needed blue blood when you had greenbacks?" Her mother's marriage to Rowen's father, a rich Irishman, had infused the family with a healthy dose of financial security if not a royal lineage.

A genuine smile slanted across Rowen's lips. This was Boston, after all, the city that gave new meaning to the phrase *melting pot.*

The steep cobbled alley that led to her front door was lit at night by gas lamps and embellished year round with overflowing flower boxes. From pansies in the spring to mums in the fall, there was always something blooming. She even managed to keep a cluster of spindly flowers alive in her own planters.

Despite the house being located in one of the city's most esteemed neighborhoods, history would not let her forget the ghosts from the past that seemingly lurked between every brick and cobblestone. She laughed dryly as she turned the key in the modern lock that secured the ancient door. Boston possessed far too much ambitious history to be considered anything but haunted. The city was the perfect backdrop for crime novels. Gritty, with gothic architecture, and as old or older than anything that could be found in this country.

Rowen tossed her keys onto the table in the entry hall. "Princess!"

There was a time when the snobby little pooch would have met her at the door. Not anymore. She waited, ensconced atop her favorite pillow on the sofa, for her master to come attend to her every need.

Rowen paused at the archway leading to the parlor. Princess lifted her head and gazed at her mistress. "Hey—"

The rest of the greeting evaporated in Rowen's throat.

The sensation of being watched, of *not* being alone was suddenly overpowering.

Instinctively, she reached for her weapon.

Princess angled her head as if to show off her pink ribbon and to say, *Why haven't you walked over here and picked me up? I'm precious and helpless.*

Slipping into cop mode, Rowen wrapped her fingers around the butt of her Glock and eased into the parlor. Princess, the useless fluff, continued to sit there and stare at her master as if she'd lost her mind or, at the very least, her good sense. She didn't even bark.

Listening for the slightest sound, Rowen stood very still for a few seconds. Maybe she'd imagined the feeling. She'd been awakened before three in the morning to go to a crime scene. It wasn't impossible that lack of sleep had her imagining things. Especially considering vampires and other ghouls were dancing in her head, screwing with her need to form impartial conclusions.

Truth was, she hadn't slept well in days. Six, to be

exact. That's how many it had taken for three young women and one man to end up dead, all from the same malady—a fatal blood donation.

The ancient hardwood floors creaked as she moved around the room, and she cringed at the sound. It wasn't as if she could memorize the spots; they changed with the climate. She focused on keeping her respiration slow and even, listening intently for any noise.

Partially closed blinds permitted minimal light to filter into the rooms. Soaring ceilings and massive pieces of dark furniture merely absorbed the sparse light and did nothing in the way of reflecting it. If she ever redecorated, *light* would be the dominant theme. Her grandmother might roll over in her grave, but Rowen would just have to take that chance.

She skirted her ancestor's massive dining table and made her way as quietly as possible toward the kitchen. Gold-trimmed china winked at her from the towering cabinet. China she never touched, much less consumed a meal from. Who had time for that kind of sit-down dinner?

The back door was secure.

The brush of a shoe sole against a carpet paralyzed her.

Upstairs.

Hallway.

Rowen swallowed tightly and moved back into the entry hall. She hesitated at the bottom of the staircase and took a deep, steadying breath.

There was no way to assess in which of the four upstairs rooms the intruder had chosen to hide, and there was only one way to find out.

She moved up the staircase in five seconds flat, incredibly without hitting the first creaky spot. The hall stood empty. The window curtains at the very end shifted in the early morning breeze, drawing Rowen's gaze there.

The intruder had entered through that window.

A flurry of anticipation shimmered along her nerve endings.

There was no doubt in her mind as to whether she had locked it or not, which meant he certainly had to have broken a pane of glass. She gritted her teeth. Antique glass. Handblown. Dammit.

Now that pissed her off. The invasion of her home was bad enough, but did the perp have to go damaging a piece of history to do it?

She took a step in that direction, her gaze sweeping from doorway to doorway, right to left and back.

"Lower your weapon."

Rowen swiveled to face the threat that had come from the landing behind her.

Her fingers tightened on the Glock. Her aim zeroed in on the intruder.

"It's me, *Rowen.*"

A fine tremor quaked through her limbs, this one not motivated by concern for her immediate safety. The bottom dropped out of her stomach and the resulting sinking sensation made her knees weak.

Evan Hunter.

She moistened her lips. Surveyed his tall frame once more just to be sure she wasn't seeing a ghost.

Wasn't he supposed to be dead?

"What're you doing here?" The question came out reflecting exactly how she felt—confused, bewildered.

"We have to talk."

She slid the safety back into the On position, then lowered her weapon as he'd requested. He didn't appear armed and she knew this man. Or, at least, she had thought she'd known him. Her palms started to sweat as more bewildering tidbits filtered into her head. She shoved the weapon back into its holster and resisted the urge to swipe her damp hands against her thighs. She didn't want him to know he'd affected her that way. Didn't want to ask the questions she desperately needed answers for. Then he would fully comprehend how much his leaving had damaged her.

Suddenly, in an abrupt moment of clarity, the full impact of the situation hit her and fury obliterated all other emotion.

She stared at the man who stood maybe four feet away. Dark glasses shielded his eyes, protected his thoughts. But she would know him anywhere. And that made her all the more furious.

She had only one thing to say to him. "Get out."

Chapter Two

It wasn't until Rowen had uttered the words, heard them echo in the thickening air, that the reality of the situation actually hit her.

This wasn't a dream—wasn't her imagination.

Evan Hunter stood only a few feet away from her.

The man who'd promised her things that hurt too badly to recall even now, three years later. The man who had walked away without looking back once. The same man she'd searched for, made endless calls about, only to learn that he'd either left his position with the FBI or he was dead. No one really knew for certain. She was a cop and hadn't even been able to find out for sure.

"I came here because you're in danger," he said quietly, as if those three years hadn't passed...as if he hadn't broken her heart beyond repair.

In that pivotal instant, the full weight of her fury broadsided her with the force of a runaway dump truck. Evan was alive. He looked whole, at least as far as she could tell with him wearing dark glasses and a long black coat that almost reached the floor.

A part of her wondered vaguely why he was dressed that way…it wasn't that cold outside.

Before any sort of reason could penetrate her mounting confusion, another, more powerful emotion regained control.

He was alive and, apparently, well and he hadn't called. Hadn't bothered to let her know that he'd simply decided not to come back.

For weeks and months, she'd grieved him. And then she'd gotten angry, made herself as well as those around her seriously miserable. Eventually she'd gotten over him. Filed away every single memory associated with him.

The idea that he would show up now—for whatever reason—was like a blast of the harsh wintry New England wind that swirled and snapped and stung as it slapped you in the face.

"I said, get out of my house."

The realization that he had broken into her home and had the audacity to stand here and toss warnings at her as if he were her assigned guardian angel made her want to shoot him on the spot. Just then, she could likely do that and not feel an inkling of remorse. Might even be able to cop a temporary insanity plea.

"Think about it, *Rowen*," he said. She'd always loved the way he said her name, with an emphasis on the second syllable—very French. "How do you suppose I gained access to your home? You're not safe here. You must—"

She held up her hands and slashed them back and forth as if she could somehow erase his words, as well as his presence. She cursed herself for the weakness the resonance of his voice could evoke. He had no right to even utter her name…not now…not after what he'd done. "Don't you dare come here after all this time, you bastard, and pretend to care what happens to me."

The anger and hurt that filled her tone was undeniable. She hated, absolutely hated, that he would know with that statement just how badly his leaving had injured her. "I don't know why you came back but I want you out of here. *Now.* Or I will call a unit to pick you up. Breaking and entering is still against the law, Hunter."

As if she hadn't spoken at all he moved closer. "Listen to me, *Rowen*," he murmured. "That's all I ask. Then if you still want to throw me out, I won't resist. Just five minutes."

She squared her shoulders and glared at him, her lips trembling in spite of her best efforts. "You don't deserve five minutes."

"I know what you think," he offered, that deep, rich timbre playing havoc with her senses, quelling her anger faster than she could reignite it. "I can't change what you think of me, but I had to come and warn you. You are in grave danger." He inclined his head as if to look beyond her to the open window. "You'll have to excuse my tactics, but I needed you to understand just how vulnerable you are."

She couldn't take this any longer. Fury driving her, she snatched the concealing eyewear from his face and forced him to look directly at her.

He squinted those pale gray eyes, held up his hand to shield them, then turned away from her, as if the dim light sifting in from the window more than a dozen yards behind her was too much to bear.

A whole new barrage of questions flooded into her brain all at once. "What's happened to you?"

It wasn't until he'd reached up to block the light that she noticed he wore gloves. Why? It was only October. Sure, the mornings could be chilly, but not that chilly.

And then what was wrong with the whole picture he presented meshed fully with her senses. His hair was far longer than before, but restrained in a ponytail. He wore all black—heavy, concealing black, including the gloves. His face looked pale…and weary.

Hunter took the glasses from her hand and slid them back into place before she could analyze anything about his eyes other than the redness that spoke of too little sleep or too much alcohol. "I didn't come here to talk about me." He settled his gaze back on her. At least, she presumed he did; the glasses once again concealed his eyes.

This was too much. Way too much. She scrubbed her hands over her face, rubbed her own eyes, then smoothed a hand over her damp hair. She needed coffee. She needed to think. She had four unsolved murders on her plate right now and she didn't need to have to deal with this, too. But she knew him…too well. There was no fighting him when he'd made up his mind about something.

Resigned to her fate, she crossed her arms defiantly. "What do you want?"

"Coffee?" The tilt of his lips could hardly be labeled a smile.

She sighed, feeling a new surge of defeat despite her challenging stance. He was here. A cup of coffee couldn't hurt. She could use one herself. Her gaze performed a tour of him once more. Some part of her, too weak or stupid to know better, needed to understand what had brought about this change in his appearance…in his manner. She shouldn't care…and yet she did.

"One cup of coffee."

He acknowledged the condition with a single nod of his dark head, then stepped aside and she led the way down the stairs. The idea that he was right behind her had goose bumps skittering over her skin. She hated that he could still do that to her. It was so damned unfair.

When they reached the entry hall Princess finally decided to bother to get up and greet the intruder.

She sniffed and yapped once. When she didn't get the desired response, she followed her mistress into the kitchen to see what would happen next.

Once Rowen got the coffee brewing, she tossed a scoop of gourmet Kibbles into the polka-dot ceramic dog food bowl and added fresh bottled water to its twin.

The dog refused to drink tap water. How was that for spoiled?

When the smell of her favorite blend of coffee had filled the air, she topped off two cups, both black. She remembered that he had taken his coffee straight up, the same as she did. It bugged the hell out of her that she could remember so much about him.

She set the cup in front of him at the small table in her cozy kitchen.

Rowen almost never ate in the dining room. Not in the past three years, anyway. She preferred the warmth and earthiness of the whitewashed cabinets and butcher-block counters. Who wanted to go to the trouble of setting a table when preparing dinner for one? That, she reminded herself, in no way diminished the fact that she was over Evan Hunter on that level. She didn't need him. Sure, he still possessed the power to make her body tremble, but there were other men out there. She simply hadn't had time to pursue a personal relationship lately.

"What's happened to you?" she asked again. She claimed the chair directly across from him so that she could appraise his face, or what she could see of it. His mouth remained fixed in a firm line, but the unflattering expression failed to lessen in any way the full, sculptured appearance of those tempting lips. Of all his assets, why the hell did she have to focus on that just then? She blinked and pushed aside the troubling notion.

"I developed a condition," he said after giving the

question lengthy deliberation, "that requires I shield my skin and eyes from light."

As he spoke, she watched his mouth move, noted the angular lines of his jaw. She'd kissed his face so many times, had reveled in his sheer beauty. As hard as she'd tried not to she'd become infatuated with him even before she'd known his name. The infatuation had given way to deeper feelings as they'd dated those few weeks. Eventually, the budding relationship had moved into serious territory. Then his work had concluded and he'd had to return to Washington.

He'd promised to call…to come back every weekend. But she'd never seen or heard from him again. Not once in three years. She'd called everyone she knew to call. Had even shown up once at the address he'd given her. A neighbor had told Rowen that she'd heard Mr. Hunter died.

That moment had served as the final straw. Rowen couldn't take anymore. She'd worked for months after that to put him behind her. It wasn't until the past year that she'd finally felt free of his irrepressible memory. Now, here he sat in her kitchen. A new trickle of ire gave way to a stream of outrage.

She braced her hands on the cool tabletop and closed her eyes. "I can't believe I'm doing this."

"*Rowen,* you must listen to me," he urged.

This was insane. She pushed up from her chair, the legs scraping across the old brick floor. "I'm sorry."

She backed away a step, needing the distance. "I can't do this."

"*Rowen*, wait—" He pushed to his feet, simultaneously reaching for her. The abrupt move jarred the table, sending both cups tumbling over and coffee sloshing across the table.

She tried to grab her cup but only succeeded in sending it spinning off the edge to crash on the rustic floor.

Swearing hotly, she turned to dive for a dish towel, but her attention jerked back to her guest. Those gloved hands had closed over his ears as if the sound of shattering stoneware had been too much for him. She'd jumped at the sound herself. The racket wasn't easy on the ears, even when one was expecting it. But this. She watched as he slowly relaxed, unclenched his jaw, took a deep breath, then lowered his hands. This was an altogether different type of reaction.

Realizing that she was staring, Rowen crouched down to gather the broken pieces of stoneware, her mind whirling with more questions. What the hell had happened to him? Was he sensitive to noise, as well as light?

"Let me help you."

He had apparently recovered enough to grab the dish towel and stoop down next to her. Her gaze lingered on him as he mopped up the mess they'd both pretty much been instrumental in making.

"Thank you." She took the towel and the broken cup and quickly disposed of them before turning her attention back to him. He waited right where she'd left him, next to the table. She should just ask the questions throbbing in her brain. He was the one who'd shown up back in her life, not vice versa. She had a right to know, didn't she?

No. Nothing he could possibly say would change what had happened.

She wasn't doing this. She would not let him drag her back down that road. "I have to get to the office." So much for coffee. She'd pick some up on the way. Right now, she just wanted out of here…away from him. "Say what you have to say and go."

Evan, with an ache still reverberating in his skull, understood why she felt this way. He'd hurt her. Memories of what they'd shared tumbled one over the other into his mind before he could stop them, adding to his misery. He'd hurt her deeply. He wasn't strong enough just now to fight the sentimental pull of that shared history. But he had to fight his personal feelings, had to try and make her see.

He ignored the pain that attempted to fragment his thoughts. Though the medication dulled his senses to a degree, he was still susceptible. Any unexpected sounds or sudden moves set off a shockwave of excruciating pain. He hated the way the medication left him off balance. But it was the only way he could tolerate the bombardment of sensations outside of his secluded home.

With her impatience mounting, he had no time for long drawn-out persuasion. Clearly, playing on her compassion wasn't working. Cutting to the chase was his only remaining option.

"You have four dead bodies," he said flatly. He had known that what he intended to propose would require a good deal more finesse, but she wasn't going to allow him the luxury. "No motive, no evidence, no acceptable manner of death."

Her gaze narrowed. "How do you know about the fourth one?"

He couldn't very well tell her that the stench of death still hung on her clothes or that her fragile emotions screamed loudly of what she'd experienced that morning. A move like that would prove detrimental to his cause. He knew Rowen…knew how she processed all that she encountered. She was already on the defensive.

"I know," was the best he could do.

Her guard moved up to the next level. Now she assessed his potential as a suspect. It was instinct. Part of what made her tick.

"What do you know about these murders?"

"I know that the *Reporter* is inciting panic."

The *Reporter* had a reputation for just this kind of exploit. For twisting the facts and magnifying the ensuing theories. But then, didn't all media do the same thing to one degree or another?

She nodded. "Vampires."

A frown marred her forehead, as if she'd only just thought of how his appearance and his sensitivity to light played into portrayals of the widely fictionalized and glamorized subject. Her heart skipped a beat before taking off into a faster rhythm, one influenced by the adrenaline filtering into her veins. He could feel her trepidation.

"But you understand that's not the case," he suggested in hopes of moving her past the topic.

She stared at him a moment, her responses slowed by her lack of sleep during the past few days. She needed to rest. But she wouldn't. She was on the case now. Rowen O'Connor was as relentless as she was meticulous.

"Do I?" she asked, countering his suggestion. She gave a little shrug. "You have no idea how I feel. You don't know me anymore, Hunter."

On that score, she was very wrong. He sensed her bitterness, the pain she felt at seeing him. But he could not allow those emotions to interfere with what had to be done. That she called him by his surname told him just how deep the cut went even if her physical reactions hadn't.

He wanted to reach out…to touch her, but he did not dare. She looked so fragile, so very vulnerable. The hasty bun into which she'd arranged her waist-length hair upon getting this morning's call had started to fall, allowing golden brown strands to drape around her shoulders. Her matching brown eyes, the color of melted caramel, looked tired, the smudges beneath testimony to her lack of sleep.

The fatigue in her slender frame vibrated beyond the confines of the tailored suit she wore. She needed him, whether she understood that just yet or not.

He could not fail. He'd risked far too much already

simply coming here. Considering her bitterness toward him, his only hope for winning her over was shock value. He had only a small window of opportunity to prove just how much he knew. He had to make her listen.

"A whole new dimension will be added to this case today," he warned. "You must be prepared for the harsh focus that will come your way almost immediately. But more treacherous is the danger to you personally. You mustn't get so caught up in the fray that your attention falters from protecting yourself. Words can't hurt you, but there are other things that can and will if you are not very, very careful, *Rowen*."

Her confusion increased as disbelief was heaped into the mixture. She didn't want to believe he'd come here to help her. Yet on some level, she knew he was telling the truth. That tiny crack in her armor left her open to having faith in him once more…gave credence to who he was when she wanted to continue despising him. Evan hated using his intimate knowledge of her for leverage, but it was, unfortunately, necessary. He, better than anyone, understood her deepest fears.

The full reality of how little regard she had for him now pierced him. The tender feelings she'd cherished were no more. When the right time came, he would tell her that she needn't waste so much energy loathing him for he already despised himself enough for the both of them.

"I have to go soon." He didn't explain the admission, simply made the statement. But he knew his limitations. The medicine would begin to wear off any minute now. Getting caught in all this—he considered the sights and sounds of the town he had once treasured simply because this is where Rowen was—would be suicide. Taking another dose this soon wouldn't be a good idea, either. "You should turn this case over to someone else, *Rowen*. Now. Today."

Rowen stood there, staring at him. His final words had rendered her speechless and immobile for what felt like an eternity. How could he possibly be aware of all these things? The man she had known three years ago had been in the business of investigating psychic phenomena. It was his job. But, above all else, he was a scientist, one employed by the FBI. The Gateway program—scientific investigation of the paranormal. To listen to him now made her feel as if the words were coming from a stranger. All of it was so very un-Hunter like.

Had he lost his mind? He, of all people, knew she couldn't—wouldn't—walk away from a case once she'd started. Changing investigators midstream would only set things back, slow down the race to nail the bastard taking innocent lives. No way would she let that happen as long as the choice was hers.

The idea that Evan Hunter had somehow developed a mental disorder from the stress associated with his work crossed her mind. That would certainly explain a lot, she decided as she surveyed him once more.

This definitely was not the man she had known, the man she'd fallen head over heels in love with. The same one who had, without a second thought, shattered her foolish heart.

Outrage solidified her courage. "Thank you for your insights, Hunter. I'll take your suggestions under advisement. But—" now or never, she had to do this "—I hope you'll understand when I say I have work to do. Thanks for dropping by."

He hesitated, didn't want to give up on whatever the hell he was trying to prove. But she couldn't deal with another moment of this. Just being in the same room with him made her ache in places she'd thought long healed.

For an entire year, she'd accepted that she was over Evan Hunter. That he was dead.

Determined to be rid of him, she put her hand to his shoulder to encourage him along. He visibly flinched. The realization that he would draw away at her touch ripped open a whole new wound. Why the hell would he show up here like this and then recoil at her touch?

"Just go," she demanded. Whatever his motivation for a personal appearance, she wasn't getting dragged into it. End of story.

Thankfully, he appeared to recognize when he was beaten and moved toward the door. His warnings kept swirling around in her head, popping up from different angles, making her wonder if he could know things she didn't.

But how was that possible?

She shook off the ridiculous concept.

Maybe, she contemplated, he was still working for the FBI.

She hesitated before opening the door, allowed her gaze to move back to his face. "If the Bureau wants in on this case, they should just say so. This kind of tactic is pointless." Proud of herself for saying the last without her voice quavering, she opened the door and waited for him to get the hell out of her house.

He didn't do so immediately, which made her want to haul out her Glock and force the issue.

"Remember what I said, *Rowen*," he reminded softly. "You must be very careful."

He walked out. Rowen watched him stride down the cobble-stoned alleyway, the sun glinting off his shiny black hair. He looked exactly like the kind of man who might have haunted these narrow streets two or three hundred years ago. The only things missing in the picture he made were the darkness and the swirling fog around his long legs. The very two items that had likely cloaked his movements as he'd entered her home via illegal means before dawn.

She shuddered and closed the door.

As if on cue, her body started to shake with the receding adrenaline.

Evan Hunter was alive.

She took two or three long, deep breaths to slow her racing heart, to calm her frazzled nerves. Why had he come back?

His warning echoed inside her. How could he know

so much about her case unless he was still involved with the FBI on some level? He couldn't. Maybe his team was investigating the murders.

But the Feds had claimed he was no longer in their service when she'd tried to find him three years ago.

She laughed dryly, bemused at the twinge of surprise the thought provoked. Why on earth was she surprised? Lies were often used as effective tools in law enforcement, from cover profiles to interrogation techniques. She'd used them herself on numerous occasions.

But this had been personal and she wasn't about to forgive Evan Hunter…no matter how good his motivation for dropping off the face of the planet.

And if the Feds were involved in her case, they'd damned well better get on board and fess up.

The chief had a contact or two. Maybe he could determine if the Bureau was snooping around in any capacity. She glanced at her watch. Dammit. She was late.

She had a date at the morgue.

The click-click-click of doggy toenails announced the arrival of Princess. She looked expectantly at Rowen.

Okay, she had a date at the morgue *after* she took Princess for a walk.

Life was all about priorities.

She thought about Carlotta Simpson and her decision, despite the threatening weather, to walk home at such an ungodly hour, thereby saving herself the fare. Death was about priorities, as well. The difference was, you didn't get a chance to regret your decisions.

Chapter Three

With a pair of latex gloves popped into place, a surgical gown pulled on over her clothes and paper covers on her hair and shoes, Rowen hesitated outside the autopsy room. She hated the powder inside the gloves that clung to her skin. Hated even worse the smell of latex. Earlier this morning, she hadn't actually had time to think about it. A murder had only just been discovered. She'd shifted into cop mode, blocked out all other thoughts to a certain degree.

But that wasn't the case now. Though there was much that could be learned from the autopsy, the actual procedure was not a part of the hands-on process for Rowen. She merely stood by and watched, listened and prayed the primary piece of evidence in any homicide, the body, would reveal useful information about the killer.

In Carlotta Simpson's situation, her body might very well be the only source of evidence. Rowen badly needed a break in this case. She needed more than the cause of death, any diseases the deceased might have had, the time, mechanism and manner of death. And yet what she needed wasn't that much.

She needed just one latent print belonging to the perp. A single piece of genetic material. Any damned thing that would connect another *human being* to this heinous act.

So she paused a moment longer outside that door, with the smell of latex making her stomach churn in warning that she should brace herself for the unpleasantness to come, and she sent one final prayer heavenward.

With another lung-expanding breath, Rowen pushed through the doors where Dr. Cost and his assistant, similarly garbed, were already deep into the procedure.

Carlotta Simpson lay on the cold steel table, nude and opened up with a Y-shaped incision for internal examination. The two tiny puncture wounds on her throat protruded in purplish rents from the gray canvas of her skin.

Dr. Cost glanced up but didn't slow in his methodical movements of removing, analyzing and weighing organs.

She didn't question him. If he'd had something for her, he would have mentioned it already.

Resignation pressed in around Rowen.

It was going to be the same thing all over again. A single victim with absolutely no clues to the perp.

The trace sheet the victim had arrived in, along with her clothes and other personal items, would already be at the crime lab. Though Rowen had been otherwise engaged and arrived later than she'd intended, she hadn't needed to be here to know that the body had already been examined for trace evidence such as hair, fibers, gunshot residue, semen, saliva and blood stains. Any findings would have been photographed, documented and collected. Clearly, in this case, there were none.

The state of rigor and the lividity—settling of the blood—were next. With this victim, like the previous three, there wouldn't be as much of the latter visible since most of the blood had been drained from the body.

Body fluids and tissues collected during this portion of the procedure would be sent out for a toxicological examination, which would reveal any detectable drugs the victim had ingested during the past several days.

As the M.E. completed his work, Rowen mentally reviewed the meager list of what she knew about this young woman. Was her murder a random act or had someone followed her from the pub? Had she known her killer? Was that the reason none of the victims' bodies had shown any indication of resistance? It struck her as odd that all four victims just happened to know their killers. The conclusion didn't feel right, and yet there were no defense wounds on any of the victims…no visible evidence that a single one of them had put up a fight for his or her life.

When Dr. Cost at last completed his task and sutured closed the incisions, it was past the lunch hour, but Rowen lacked any appetite. After a long period of silence, the M.E. turned to her as if what he had to say had only just occurred to him. "I have two things to show you, Detective."

Rowen moved to a higher state of alert. She hoped like hell this would be the break they needed.

Cost directed her attention to the victim's left arm. "She had apparently donated to the Red Cross recently. The puncture is consistent with the gauge of needle used."

Rowen nodded. That would be easy enough to verify.

"Now for the coup de grâce," Cost said mysteriously. With his assistant's help, he rolled the body to one side enough to show a tattoo on the right hip. A white, open-bloom flower about the size of a quarter.

Rowen studied the flower but didn't recognize it. Kind of like a…then she realized what it was: a dogwood blossom. "Have you seen this particular flower used as a symbol before?" She was certain she hadn't, other than as related to the tree or maybe as a religious symbol of some sort.

"Look closer." Cost offered her a magnifying glass.

Rowen peered through the handheld magnifier, studied the bloom with its detailed petals. Her breath caught as she noted the bluish letters glimmering beneath the white of the petals.

"Do you see what it spells?"

The anticipation in Dr. Cost's voice lit a matching one in her veins.

D…O…N…O…R.

Donor?

"Do you recognize this as a particular symbol?" Rowen set the magnifying glass aside and fixed her attention on the M.E. He was practically beaming, he was so proud of himself. She wasn't aware of any sort of similar symbol used by those who donated to Red Cross on a regular basis. "Don't keep me in suspense, Doc." She had already pretty much maxed out her stress level for the day. And it was taking every ounce of willpower she possessed not to mentally go down that Transylvania bloodsucker avenue right now. With that thought came images of Hunter's strange appearance, which she immediately booted out.

He peeled off the clean gloves he'd tugged on after the messier part of his work. "Come, you'll see."

Behaving even more puzzlingly, Cost led her over to a computer occupying a large portion of the counter space on a worktable on the other side of the room. He tapped a few keys and the image Rowen had seen on the victim's hip appeared on the screen.

Another tap of the keys and an explanation of one use of the image popped up next.

Rowen read, hardly believing her eyes.

The symbol was used to mark donors belonging to a certain so-called cult. The same damned one she'd been working so hard to mentally detour. Vampires.

She turned to meet Cost's waiting gaze. "What do you make of that?" She knew what she'd read, but she wanted to hear what the M.E. had to say first. In the back of her mind, Hunter's warning that a new dimension would be added to this case whispered, vying for her attention.

"I think this is a lead, Detective." He scrubbed at his stubbled chin. "Our first in this case. Not that I believe in vampires, but there are those who do. Clearly."

Rowen nodded. She had to agree. There were those who believed in creatures of the night and this certainly fell into the category of a break in a case that had until now been going nowhere.

But this…she looked back at the screen…this wasn't the kind of break she'd been hoping to get. Then again, beggars couldn't be choosers.

"I need to find out where she got this tattoo." She would need a picture of the one on the victim's body.

Having anticipated her requirement, Cost picked up a handful of pages from the printer and passed them to her. The digital image of Carlotta Simpson's tattooed hip covered the first page. The second and third were the generic image and accompanying description Rowen had viewed on the doc's computer screen, both likely garnered from research on the Internet.

Going back to the chief with something, as bizarre as this might be, was better than going back with nothing, she supposed. But he wasn't going to like this. Not one little bit.

"Thanks, Doc." She produced a smile for the M.E. "Let me know if anything useful shows up in toxicology."

Cost assured her that she would be the first to hear from him. Having received that promise, Rowen headed back to the office. She needed to brief the chief and touch base with her partner. Hopefully he would have more details on the victim, such as who her next of kin were.

They finally had a lead. Maybe a dead-end one, but it was something to move forward on just the same. Nothing like this had been found on any of the other victims, so the tattoo might not even relate to the murder.

Carlotta Simpson either was or had been a *donor.* If the Internet source could be trusted, a secret society of ordinary humans who provided a regular, fresh supply of blood in a relationship that had nothing to do with the venerable Red Cross.

The benefactors were self-proclaimed vampires.

AT ONE SCHROEDER PLAZA, Rowen parked and entered the sleek, modern complex that housed all branches of the Boston PD, as well as a crime lab. A massive marble-floored lobby with soaring windows and skylights welcomed all those who entered. Though the building was now nearly a decade old and beginning to show a little wear and tear, it still beat the hell out of most cops' digs.

She glanced back one last time before boarding the elevator. Even now, even here, she felt as if someone watched her every move.

Lack of sleep, she told herself again. Those same old nightmares that had haunted her when Hunter first walked out on her appeared to be back. Just in time for his visit. Wasn't that nice?

Despite her bitter feelings toward him, she refused to consider that he was stalking her. He wasn't that kind of guy…not that she wanted to take his side in any form or fashion. The idea of how he'd looked…how he'd reacted to the noise from the cup breaking poked into her confusing thoughts next. There was something very wrong about his demeanor.

Shaking off the speculations, she stepped out of the elevator and surveyed her home away from home. The Boston Homicide Division, with its carpeted floors and contemporary workstations, offered the same conveniences of a swanky corporate office. Not shabby at all.

Chief Bart Koppel wouldn't want to hear anything about vampires, but Rowen went straight to his office and gave him what she had, just the same.

"If the media gets wind of this, we'll have mass hysteria on our hands. Not to mention we'll both likely be committed." He flung his arms outward in disgust, then paced the length of the room once more. At fifty, the chief generally looked young for his age. But not today. Today, he looked every day of those fifty years. His salt-and-pepper hair lacked its usual sheen and perfectly coiffed style. And the elegant suit looked rumpled rather than sophisticated. Even his tie looked like it had scoliosis.

Koppel had been her chief from day one. She trusted and admired him. He'd gone through a rough patch a few years back when his wife had died, but he'd slowly gotten back to being himself. He was one of the good guys. A nice guy who had a big office with a nice view.

He wanted to keep it, but the South End Murders were bringing major pressure down on him. He, in turn, was pushing as much of it as possible in Rowen's direction. She was the lead detective, after all.

Dirty business always rolled downhill.

"I'll keep this to myself for now," Rowen allowed, in keeping with his roundabout suggestion. "See what I can find and let the others concentrate on family and friends of the latest vic."

By others, she meant her partner, Detective Merv Gant, and Detective Lenny Doherty. She'd partnered with Merv about three years ago, around the same time Hunter came into her life. Lenny had been around longer. His partner had recently retired and he hadn't been assigned anyone new yet. The chief had put him with Rowen and Merv as soon as the third body in the South End Murders had been discovered.

Any minute now, a full-fledged task force would be launched. The chief, as did Rowen, wanted this case solved before it escalated to that point.

"Keep me posted, Detective," Koppel reminded before letting her go. "I've got a bad feeling this one's going to get ugly and you and I are going to be caught smack in the middle of the witch hunt."

He was right. A reasonable explanation and satisfying resolution were required posthaste. Without one or both, heads would roll.

Rowen almost walked out of his office without asking the question that, in spite of the other pressing issue, nagged her. She couldn't let the possibility go that easily. "Chief, do you know of any Bureau investigation related to this case?"

The chief, who'd only just relaxed back into his leather executive chair, sat up straighter, looked suspicious or nervous or maybe both. "What do you mean, O'Connor? Has someone contacted you?"

She shook her head, not deeming the response an actual lie. Hunter hadn't mentioned any affiliation with the Bureau. He'd claimed his visit was purely personal. But she couldn't be sure.

"I just wondered if the Feds might try horning in at this point. You know, with the media hype." That's when they usually made an appearance. Not that she would resent the help. God knew she didn't want any more senseless deaths. If a joint task force would get this done, she was all for it.

"I'll nudge a few of my sources," the chief promised and she left it at that.

Rowen made her way to her workstation, hoping she wouldn't run into anyone en route who wanted to talk. She needed to focus for a while. To get this morning's murder into perspective and to get her unexpected visitor out of her head. Not such an effortless task, and that infuriated her all the more. More important, she didn't want to field any questions from the other detectives, her partner in particular.

She and her partner had been through the steps on this one already. Both knew their jobs. The psychiatrist Boston PD relied upon for analysis in cases like this had worked up a psychological profile. Every possible angle was being considered, for all the good it appeared to be doing.

How did one profile a vampire?

Not funny, she mused.

It didn't take long for Rowen to get buried deeply enough in her work to cast Hunter into some rarely visited area of gray matter. She'd almost completely forgotten him by the time the phone on her desk rang and interrupted her research into local tattoo parlors and recent Red Cross hits in the area of the latest victim's workplace and residence.

"O'Connor."

"Detective Rowen O'Connor?"

Rowen sat back in her chair, her instincts automatically going on point. She didn't know the caller's name yet, but there was something about his voice that struck a chord akin to fear deep inside her. Images from the nightmares she suffered all too often flickered like a short in a dilapidated neon sign.

Shaking off the foolish reaction, she confirmed, "This is Detective O'Connor."

"I think we need to talk, Detective."

She checked the caller ID on her phone, noting a blocked number.

"Identify yourself, sir."

If this was a prank call…

"My name is Viktor Azariel. If you have a pen, I'll give you my address."

There was something about his voice, something intriguing and yet dangerous. Commanding. And strangely familiar. Who the hell was this man?

"I'm sorry, Mr. Azariel. We haven't clarified that I need your address. What's the nature of your call?"

"You are Detective Rowen O'Connor," he reiterated. "The lead investigator in the South End Murders?"

"Yes." Her patience was running thin now. Wasn't someone supposed to be screening out the crazies? Ever since that *Reporter* article hit the newsstands, hundreds of nuts had called in vampire sightings. Hell, a half dozen or so had confessed!

"Then we do, indeed, need to speak, Detective. Today. *Now,* if at all possible."

Rowen's fingers tightened around the receiver, but a gut feeling she couldn't deny kept her from hanging up on the guy. "You'll have to be more specific, sir," she said, pressing for something that would give her a hint as to whether or not this guy was just another loony.

"Your latest victim," he said in that deep, peculiarly alluring tone that sent a shiver over her nerve endings, "her name was Carlotta Simpson, no?"

Now he had her attention. Who the hell was this guy? Miss Simpson's face had already been splashed all over the news despite the police's inability to contact next of kin. A nosy neighbor had seen to that. But having any aspect of the case verified by a member of Boston PD was another thing altogether.

"Miss Simpson was one of mine," the gentleman said frankly.

Confusion slowed Rowen's response, had another wave of uncertainty seeping into her bones. "One of yours? I'm not sure I'm following, Mr… What did you say your name was again?" She readied her pen to write this time.

"Viktor Azariel." He spelled both first and last just to be sure she got it.

"In what way were you connected to the victim, Mr. Azariel?" Rowen slipped that one in on him in an effort to catch him off guard.

"She was one of my donors, Detective. Now, would you like my address?"

THE DRIVE to the Berkshires, home to some of the most beautiful and historic homes in western Massachusetts, was always pleasant. Rowen had to admit there was something intensely relaxing about getting away from the congestion of the city.

But then the flyers and billboards posted everywhere she looked drew her right back to what she wanted to forget. Salem witch trials…vampires in Boston. Happy Halloween. New England tourism depended a great deal on what the changing fall colors, as well as the area's haunting history, could bring in. All of it served as the perfectly *wrong* backdrop for her case. She didn't need these exaggerations filtering into her investigation.

Putting the ghoulish holiday and all it entailed aside,

the weather was perfect and she couldn't help but enjoy the blue sky she rarely saw when on a case. No wonder those who could left work in the city and came here to call someplace home.

But that Prozac-like feeling of serenity came with a megabuck price tag. If you didn't have it, don't bother. Not unlike Martha's Vineyard and the Hamptons, the good life in the Berkshires was reserved for the rich and powerful. Or at least for those with unlimited credit lines.

Like many of the affluent residents of the area, Mr. Viktor Azariel had opted for big when building his home. The place was, in fact, a castle. The structure sat in the distance, on a hillside no less, as she approached the turnoff to the property. And she didn't mean the modern fabricated castle a few in the area had erected in recent years. Nope. Mr. Azariel had purchased his castle in Europe and had the centuries-old structure shipped to the property stone by stone. She found an article on the Net related to the ambitious move. An actual fifteenth-century English Gothic-style manor.

Rowen stopped at the gate to the seventy-five-acre property and showed her ID. The guard waved her through without fanfare. Coming alone had been her decision. Too much ground needed to be covered to drag Merv or Lenny away from their work.

As she moved down the long, winding drive, the lush landscape made even a New England born and bred girl sit up and take notice. Forests flanked the property on either side. The leaves had started to turn their fall colors—amber, russet and gold. The final bend in the drive took her upward and to the open area where the grand castle made an exhilarating in-your-face appearance. Rowen slowed to a stop and just sat there and stared. An immense Tiffany glass window depicted a vivid scene with brilliant colors that stood out in stark relief against the cloudy granite and aged limestone of the monstrosity. A gargoyle would have looked right at home climbing the soaring tower from which one could likely see all the way to Martha's Vineyard.

"Holy crap," she muttered.

She'd done a little research on Viktor Azariel. He was listed as the chief investor of a pharmaceutical research corporation, a Fortune 500 company. He was called a recluse by the two reporters who had been allowed to interview him in the past decade and he refused to have his photograph taken. He had no wife or kids, no family at all as far as anyone had been able to ascertain.

Obviously whatever he was doing paid extremely well. A Bentley sat in the curved drive near a fountain that likely cost more than her home.

A well-dressed gentleman waited for Rowen on the steps. She emerged from the car and wondered as she did if this was Mr. Azariel.

"This way, Detective O'Connor."

Since he didn't introduce himself as the lord of the manor, she assumed he was the butler or other hired help. She hadn't actually expected the kazillionaire Azariel to meet her on the steps of his castle.

Once she stepped through those massive bronze entry doors, the ambience completely changed. Rowen was taken aback by the sharp contrast. Outside had been lush and sunny, bright and lovely. All that one would expect in the setting for a lavish estate.

None of those adjectives could be used to describe the interior. The entry hall was cavernous, the decor, as well as the furnishings, minimal. Even the elegant Tiffany glass of the massive window overlooking the entry hall was darkened by a tapestry. The lighting was meager at best. She felt as though she had stepped onto an alien planet. A weight pressed in around her, as if she'd entered a totally different atmosphere. The air felt thicker…danker.

And it was so cold. Rowen shivered.

Yet, the raw beauty of the marble and limestone suggested it had been hand-chiseled by Italian sculptors. The detailed oaken trim might have been crafted by Bavarian wood-carvers. Truly amazing.

"Mr. Azariel will be with you shortly."

The man, butler, whoever, who had not identified himself, waited near another set of massive wood doors. These, too, were intricately detailed. He held one door open, an eerie Norman Bates smile plastered on his lips, and waited for her to enter. She hurried to catch up since she'd fallen a little behind in an attempt to take in and analyze what she'd encountered.

"Thank you."

He nodded before closing the door behind her, leaving her alone in another less than ergonomically inviting space.

The room she'd been sequestered in appeared to be a parlor or study, though there wasn't a desk around anywhere. God knew, the room was big enough to hold the entire Homicide Division. A couple of chairs and two settee-type sofas sat near the enormous stone fireplace. A sideboard sat against one wall. The floors were stone, as well. The whole theme was austere and cold.

Rowen shivered again and wondered why a man with such means would choose to live so spartanly…

"Thank you for coming, Detective."

Rowen spun to face the man who'd come into the room without her realizing it. She hadn't heard the door open or close. Usually she was much more astute and aware of her surroundings.

Summoning her wits, she strode straight up to him and stuck out her hand. "Mr. Azariel. I'm Rowen O'Connor, homicide division."

For several moments, he stared at her hand as if he wasn't sure whether he wanted to touch it. Rowen wondered if that was merely one of his reclusive traits. Any one of a number of phobias that instantly came to mind often caused those who could afford the luxury to go into seclusion.

While he assessed her proffered gesture, she assessed him. Tall, six-three or -four. Broad-shouldered, but not overly large, more lean and muscled versus bulky. His dark hair was long, fell around his shoulders. He wore a white shirt, plain but expensive. Black trousers, but clearly not the kind one would find on the rack. Black leather boots.

His hand abruptly closed around hers and all thought fled her consciousness.

"I am Viktor Azariel."

His eyes, black as soot, drew her in, hypnotized her.

Rowen blinked, tried to regain her bearings, but there was something about his eyes, combined with his touch, that rattled her.

One swift downward sweep of his dark lashes and the spell was broken. He drew back his hand and the moment dissolved like so much smoke in a sudden gale. Rowen's hand dropped to her side.

Okay, this was not a normal response for her. She struggled to catch the breath that had somehow escaped her without her realizing it. Not enough sleep, she reasoned for the dozenth time. Hunter's unexpected arrival had likely left her off her game.

"You wanted to talk?" The words lacked the strength and conviction she usually conveyed, but she'd gotten the question out and, for now, that was all that mattered.

"Please." He indicated the sofas near the fireplace. "Sit down, won't you?"

Rowen decided that sitting might be a good thing considering how weak her knees felt at the moment. She turned away from the man and walked over to take a seat. The idea that he followed, probably measuring her from a whole other perspective, only made bad matters worse.

She sat down on the luxuriously upholstered sofa and waited for her host to do the same. Thankfully, he chose to sit opposite her. And in spite of the fact that a polished wood table spanned the distance between them and they were on equal footing, so to speak, since he no longer towered over her, his presence still intimidated Rowen on a level she couldn't quite rationalize. She couldn't remember the last time she'd felt so dominated by anyone.

"Carlotta Simpson was one of my donors," he said, drawing her attention back to the matter at hand. "I wanted to make myself available to you in the event I could help in some way to bring her murderer to justice."

As she made the trip from Boston proper to the countryside, Rowen had considered what Mr. Azariel hoped to offer to her investigation. She'd mulled over the possibilities of what sort of relationship he and the deceased had maintained and came up with a couple of possibilities. Perhaps Miss Simpson had served as a paid participant in drug tests, the kind where some people actually received a drug and others a placebo. She might have donated, so to speak, blood, eggs, who knew? But that was the route Rowen's thoughts on the matter had taken.

"You obviously feel you have something to contribute to the investigation," she prompted, trying to maintain her boundaries.

If she got even a fleeting glimmer that he intended to drag this meeting into that dark theory the *Reporter* had thrown out to the masses, he could forget it. She had her orders, straight from the chief.

"As I told you on the telephone," he began, in that accent she couldn't quite pinpoint, a mixture of British formality and French irreverence, "Miss Simpson is—was—one of my donors."

Okay, there was that word. Rowen restrained the urge to shift with her mounting uneasiness.

"Again, Mr. Azariel, I need you to be more specific. What sort of donor was Miss Simpson?"

He inclined his head, that dark hair falling to one side, revealing the sharp angles of his face and making her gut clench unreasonably.

"You saw the mark, no?"

She tensed. The idea that this could be a trick to get her to spill details that had not been released to the press had already crossed her mind. Those same warning bells were clanging big-time right now.

"What mark do you mean?" Rowen worked hard to keep her face devoid of emotion, her eyes clear of her thoughts.

"Let's not waste time, Detective," he said bluntly, those unfathomably dark eyes boring into hers, "the flower on her right hip. A dogwood blossom with her designation embedded within the design."

Rowen swallowed, resisted the urge to rush forward with the questions crowding into her brain. She had to tread carefully here, couldn't allow him to see that he'd nailed her one lead. "Are you certain we're talking about the same woman? Simpson is not exactly an uncommon name. Your *donor* may—"

Viktor Azariel ticked off every single detail Rowen knew about Carlotta Simpson. Including some she didn't, such as the fact that she had no siblings, her parents were both deceased and that she had an appointment with a talent agent in New York the next week. One she obviously wouldn't be keeping.

At that precise moment, her cell phone rang. Rowen took a breath to fill her empty lungs. "Excuse me."

Needing distance, she stood and moved to the far side of the room. As she dug the cell phone from her jacket pocket, she resisted the urge to draw open the drapes to allow some sunlight to fill the dimly lit room.

"O'Connor."

"Ro, I got some info on the Simpson family."

It was Merv, her partner. "Great. Let's have it." She told herself that his call was coincidence. Even considered that perhaps the distraction could be helpful to her at the moment.

"Her parents died in a fire in their Galveston apartment seven years ago. Carlotta was spending the night with a friend. No siblings. She came to Boston for college two years ago. I'm still working on a list of friends from school. Her boss said she was pretty much a loner at work."

"Thanks, Merv. I'll touch base with you later."

Rowen closed her phone and stashed it back in her pocket. She blanked her face and shored up her defenses before turning back to her host.

"Sorry for the interruption," she said as she joined him once more.

Those dark eyes settled on hers, but he said nothing. There was the slightest hint of smugness in his expression, as if he knew what her partner had called about. Not possible.

"Let's cut to the chase, Mr. Azariel." Beating around the bush had never been her style—unless, of course, it served her needs. "What sort of donor was Miss Simpson? She worked for your corporation in some capacity?"

For several seconds, Rowen was certain he didn't intend to answer, but then he surprised her and gave her more than she'd asked for.

"You don't want to know the truth, Detective, but I'm going to give it to you for my own reasons."

He had to be guessing, putting together the recent headlines and her uneasiness. No good cop ever wanted to deal with crap like vampires in the mist. And that's what he had to be hinting at. She shuddered inwardly as she considered her current surroundings. Oddly, the man, the place, it all fit too damned well.

"Miss Simpson donated to my thirst. Without such generous souls, my life would not be tolerable."

They'd just crossed that boundary she'd wanted to avoid.

And now there was no going back.

Chapter Four

The night teemed with activity, but it was far from the crowded rush, the blare of horns and scream of a thousand voices filling the daylight hours.

It had been three long years since Evan had allowed himself to walk the streets of any city.

But tonight he had no choice but to take the risk.

After hours of isolation and a second round of medication, he felt braced for the onslaught. He wore his darkest shades. Shielded himself with dark clothing that concealed most of his body.

He would have to work quickly. Long-term use of the drug was detrimental, if not outright dangerous, considering the side effects, not the least of which was its extreme addictive quality. Despite the inherent hazards, the numbing effects only postponed the agony. But his options were sorely limited.

Three years ago, his team had come to Boston to investigate reports of increased cult activity involving vampirism. Their investigation had revealed nothing but the usual pop culture fanatics.

With the exception of one group.

Evan stood in the shadows at the mouth of the alley where Carlotta Simpson had died. Strips of crime scene tape hung across the opening but he ignored it, stepped cautiously over the sagging barrier and disappeared into the darkness.

He sniffed the air, smelled the essence of death that still lingered there. The medication had little effect on his sense of smell. If anything, with his other senses dulled, that one became even keener.

He leaned against the cooling brick and closed his eyes, allowed the sensations to wash over him. A tremor of fear went through him, making his lungs expel the breath he'd just taken. Carlotta Simpson had known she was being followed. Her fear still echoed in the air like the wail of a distant foghorn. She'd hurried through the darkness as black fingers of horror clawed through the mist that rolled in to fill the vacant path she'd left behind.

Evan opened his eyes and surveyed the alley on either side of him. Nothing moved. No sound. No presence other than his own. Yet someone was aware.

He knew Evan was here, in Boston.

And he'd already taken steps to gain himself some negotiable leverage.

Evan had hoped to intervene quickly enough to prevent Rowen's involvement with the evil bastard, but it was too late now.

That overwhelming sense of doom he'd felt for weeks attempted to cloud his focus. He pushed it aside. It was true he had been out of the field for three years, but he had not forgotten his training, the decade of experience. He was not the one who should be afraid this night.

The air grew thicker, colder, or perhaps it was Evan's most deeply entrenched instincts warning him that company was close at hand. A drizzling rain started to fall like tears for the murdered woman whose essence still lingered here in this dark, lonely place.

A ripple in the fabric of the night announced the coming of the one Evan had known would appear sooner or later.

Viktor Azariel materialized from the shadows a few yards away, his silk cape wafting behind him as he strode toward the spot where Carlotta Simpson's body had been found. His intense focus on his goal left him blind to Evan's presence.

As Evan watched, Viktor knelt and touched the tainted ground where the woman had fallen. He hovered there for many minutes as rage mounted inside him.

Well, that answered one of Evan's questions.

Viktor Azariel had not murdered the young woman whose life had been drained from her barely twenty-four hours ago in this desolate alley.

Viktor's head came up, his gaze luminous with his fury.

"Hunter." He lunged to his feet and adopted a battle-ready stance. "Why have you come here?" Beyond the rage, there was a vulnerability in him. This woman had meant something to him.

Evan stepped away from the wall and its cloaking shadow, moved closer to his enemy. That Viktor had not killed Carlotta Simpson or that he had suffered because of her death did not change his status in Evan's opinion.

"You swore you would keep your people under control," Evan said, his tone low but unquestionably lethal. "That is the only reason you were allowed to live."

His extreme rage making him more daring, Viktor stepped closer. "You speak of death as if only you have the power to wield it. I could kill you right now, Hunter, if the desire struck me," he sneered. "Do not think that our history will influence my need for revenge. That would be a supreme mistake."

One corner of Evan's mouth twitched with the need to smile at the bastard's audacity. "You won't kill me, Viktor. We both know that. So save the theatrics for someone more easily impressed by the performance."

With a single blink of his eyes, the clever nightwalker concealed his violent emotions. "I trust this case is of some significance to you or your precious team?"

Now it was Evan's turn to flaunt his fury. His fingers curled with the need to end this now. To do what he should have done three years ago. "You know why this case carries significance for me. You also know damned well that every member of my team is dead except me."

A smirk of triumph spread across that too pale

face. "Ah…but you're wrong, my old friend. You are dead in many ways, as well. You simply haven't admitted it yet."

Evan resisted the increasing urge to tear out his throat. "Enough reminiscing. I have questions. You will provide the answers."

"You think so?" Viktor taunted as he assessed the threat Evan presented on a physical level. "Don't misjudge your powers of persuasion, my old friend. Much has changed in three years. More than you can possibly know."

Evan didn't really give a damn what had changed in Viktor's dark world. His only concern was for Rowen. Instinct had already warned him that Viktor had not come alone. Others gathered in the shadows even now.

"Have some of your followers gone rogue?"

Viktor laughed; the sound bounced off the crumbling brick walls, sent shards of pain through Evan's brain.

"Not one of my breed would dare touch a human designated as my personal donor," he said fiercely. "This was not the work of my kind."

"How can you be so sure, Viktor? Perhaps competition has moved in from the west coast. Reliable donors have become difficult to find there."

Viktor suddenly reached out, cupped the back of Evan's head and jerked him nearer. That penetrating gaze locked in, searching, analyzing. Had the medication not dulled Evan's senses so, his nemesis would not have managed such a feat.

The fingers of Evan's right hand closed around the other man's throat, sinking harshly into the vulnerable flesh there. "Back off," Evan growled.

The self-proclaimed vampire royal continued to stare, ignoring the command and soaking in all that his powerful senses told him.

"You have been gravely damaged, Hunter," he said softly, before letting go. Evan's own fingers loosened and his enemy took a step back.

He looked wholly unrepentant. "The drugs are killing you at this very moment and yet here you are."

"I want to know who is behind these murders." Evan struggled to keep his thoughts and emotions tightly compartmentalized. He knew that with the physical connection Viktor had made, he would work all the harder to see Evan's every thought. The man had immense power when it came to sensing the weaknesses of others, there was no question there.

"And you think I do not?" Viktor tossed the question right back at him. "I will have my revenge. My kind does not need this attention."

"Stay away from *Rowen*," Evan warned, getting directly to the point. "She doesn't have the answers you seek. I think you know that."

Viktor smiled. "Ah, but she does have one thing that I desire very much."

Evan's gaze narrowed with suspicion as a new wave of fury flamed inside him. "Go near her and I will end your pathetic existence."

"She has immense power over you, my old friend, and that is my greatest desire just now."

Evan went toe-to-toe with him. "Don't go near her again. That is your final warning."

Viktor merely looked at him, unfazed by the blatant intimidation tactic. "But you see, Hunter, I won't have to go to her. She will come to me. You must know that." Again his lips stretched into that facsimile of a smile that held not even a glimmer of compassion. "That's what terrifies you." With that confident announcement, the soulless son of a bitch turned and walked away.

That truth rang in his ears as Evan watched him fade into the night.

Before this investigation was over, one of them would have to die. Their unlikely alliance had gone on too long already.

Evan stared up at the sky. Only a few more good hours left before the harsh glare of day would drive him back into isolation. His senses were already overtaxed from the encounter with Viktor.

But there was still work to be done. He would visit each crime scene and absorb all that he could before returning to his temporary sanctuary.

Sometime during the coming day, he would have to talk to Rowen again.

He had to make her understand how dangerous Viktor Azariel was. She could not trust him. He would not help her with this investigation. Viktor had an agenda of his own. He would stop at nothing to accomplish it.

Indulging his primal needs, Evan closed his eyes and envisioned Rowen asleep in her bed—the gauzy white gown nestled against her skin, her honey-colored hair spread across her pillow. That intense sensation of imminent doom banded around his chest once more and a surge of clarity struck. Somehow this investigation was destined to bring him here…to draw Rowen to this place.

What was it about these murders that had brought the three of them together? Rowen, Viktor and him? Something about their shared pasts. A connection that he couldn't yet see.

He had to learn what that connection was before Rowen got any closer to Viktor. There were things she had forgotten. Things she could never know.

ROWEN DREAMED of a dark castle.

A place cold and dank where something forbidding waited around every corner.

She could hear his voice…calling to her through the darkness. She tried to answer but couldn't speak.

Why was she there? Was he after her?

She felt the brush of evil against her skin…groped for safety but found none.

Terror welled in her heart, but she couldn't scream. Couldn't run. Her feet were mired in the floor that suddenly evolved into a threatening, pulsing quicksand. She could only stand there and let one danger come closer and closer while the other engulfed her with a confusing mixture of fear and anticipation.

Evan suddenly swooped her into his arms and took her to safety. She looked into his eyes and saw the love she'd thought she'd seen three years ago. Found reflected there the same feelings she still carried for him.

His image suddenly morphed into another, less familiar one.

Long dark hair fell around broad shoulders, black eyes stared longingly at her.

The blood started to drain out of her. She wrapped her hands around her throat…tried to stop it but it was no use. It poured out of her in a river of red.

Rowen bolted upright in bed. Her breath sawed in and out of her lungs. Perspiration dampened her skin, and her heart threatened to burst from her chest.

She flung the covers back and scrambled out of the bed. She recognized the symptoms. Panic attack. She had to walk this off.

Her fingers went immediately to her throat…just to be sure.

She shouldn't be letting the case get to her like this. She was letting the whole crazy vampire theory creep under her skin. But the dreams…they were nothing new. The only difference was that the shadowy figures in her nightmares had taken on the faces of those who'd recently barged into her life. And somehow they fit. She shuddered inwardly.

Feeling her way to the bathroom, she went in search of water. Her throat was dry and tight. She stuck her head under the faucet and drank deeply, then straightened and wiped her mouth with a trembling hand.

Back in her bedroom, she switched on the bedside lamp and retrieved her Glock from under her pillow. Princess lifted her dainty head from the pillow next to Rowen's long enough to gaze sleepily at the disturbance, but she made no move to join her mistress in her middle-of-the-night ramblings. Unlike Rowen, Princess apparently preferred her beauty sleep.

Her weapon in hand, for reasons she refused to consider, Rowen moved down the stairs, not bothering with additional light. A small night-light in the entry hall provided sufficient illumination for her to make her way down the staircase. She actually could have done it with her eyes closed. Her grandmother used to make a game of walking around the house blindfolded. She insisted that it made her more aware of her surroundings. Rowen felt confident it was more likely a ruse to ensure she paid attention to her movements in the house after that one scary tumble she'd taken down the stairs when she was five.

Rowen's fingers glided down the railing, the sensation bringing back a collage of memories and stories her grandmother had told. Many lives, she had boasted, had come and gone in this house. A house couldn't stand so long without having a few ghosts pass through and maybe even a few linger. Just like Boston, nothing got that old without some accumulated baggage. Alleged hauntings…legends of hanging witches in the Common. All of it, combined with the distinctive old Boston flavor, made for ripe fodder for overactive imaginations.

Rowen's feet landed on the cool wooden floor of the entry hall as she descended the final step. Not that she believed in ghosts per se, but she did believe that those who'd come before left an energy or an essence in the air for those sensitive enough to notice. That explained why some folks insisted they saw ghosts. What they actually encountered were memories built over time, the way the moisture in the air accumulated until the clouds were heavy enough to send it returning to Earth in the form of rain. The rising vapor had been there all along; you just hadn't been able to see it until it took liquid form. Hunter had shared that analogy with her. He believed that our world was made up of layers of time, each carrying its own residue.

Don't even think about him, she chastised. Don't let him sneak back in.

She paused in front of the window over the kitchen sink and watched the rain trickle down the wavy glass. If there had been a speck of evidence left at the Simpson crime scene, it would be long gone now.

The angels were crying for those who'd lost their lives, Rowen decided. It had rained every damned day since the murders began…tears from heaven.

But there really wasn't a legitimate reason to fret about the storm contaminating anything useful. She shivered. There hadn't been any evidence to find. That was this killer's MO, it seemed. His ability to get away so clean could very well mean he knew his way around a crime scene. God, she hated even the idea of that scenario. But she had to consider all possibilities. This killer could be a former cop…maybe even a cop still on active duty.

Or it could be Hunter.

Another shudder quaked through her limbs.

Looking at the glass, she suddenly remembered that the window he had opened remained intact. She knew she'd locked it. It was always locked. But somehow he'd managed to open it without damaging the antique glass. Or maybe he'd picked the lock on one of the doors and opened the window to throw her off.

No matter how he'd gained entrance, it made her damned mad. She'd always felt safe here and he had taken that away from her. Was that the reason for tonight's strange nightmare? Was she feeling she was losing control? The nightmares had always come when she felt some aspect of her life was out of her sphere of power. She recognized that particular frailty about herself.

No, she decided. Viktor Azariel was the culprit here. She shivered again, hugged her arms around herself, feeling comforted by the cold, hard steel of the Glock.

Mr. Azariel had, without hesitation, explained that he was a vampire and Carlotta, who was one among many, had regularly donated blood for his thirst.

Rowen had pretty much gotten the hell out of there after that. He hadn't told her anything about the Simpson woman that Merv, her partner, hadn't discovered. So the trip had been more or less wasted.

No, that wasn't true. She just hadn't learned anything she could say to the public in hopes of assuaging their mounting concerns.

Not in this lifetime.

It was bad enough that the *Reporter* was now running a series of articles related to vampires and the connection to All Hallows' Eve. The timing on all this was just too perfect. Fate had played a really bad trick on her this time. Along with the usual fall and Halloween revelers pouring into Boston was a whole other fan club. Vampire lovers, even some who professed to be vampires themselves, were filling up the hotels in hopes of getting a front row seat for this ugly sideshow.

Rowen shook her head in disgust.

But what Viktor Azariel had done, whether he knew it or not, was give her another avenue to legitimately delve into. The chief didn't want to discuss the possibility that self-professed vampires lived anywhere near his city. He'd have to get past that—the facts were the facts. Vampirism was a wildly popular cult. Not all vampire wanna-bes actually partook of blood, but some did.

She decided that Viktor Azariel fit neatly into that second category.

The blood, since it hadn't made him ill, obviously gave him a feeling of power, of superiority. That part wasn't really surprising. There were medical treatments that involved blood derivatives that promoted health and well-being. But those treatments involved extensive testing and, often, matching donor to recipient.

She'd chalked up Azariel's perceptiveness as to where she was on the investigation to guesswork since he couldn't have known how far along she was on Simpson's autopsy results or her investigation into the donor emblem. But he still gave her the creeps.

A quiver skittered up her spine at the idea of just how far he'd taken the whole I'm-cursed act. With his money, the man could have anything. Had he grown so bored with all that money could buy that he sought fulfillment in horror fantasy? Would he actually risk his health by drinking the blood of others?

Apparently, he did.

Admittedly, there was something sexy about dark and dangerous men. That's what had attracted her to Hunter. Viktor Azariel possessed the same sort of seductive qualities. She wasn't blind.

But he was clearly a few bricks short of a load.

"Seriously mental," she murmured.

Rowen reached into the fridge and grabbed a power drink. She was awake. Might as well make the most of it and get some work done. She wanted to do a little more research on the whole I-think-I'm-a-vampire religion and see if she could find any suggestion of hypnosis being utilized. That appeared to be the most likely scenario since none of the victims had fought off their attackers and no drugs had shown up in their tox screens.

She closed the fridge door, blinked a couple of times to readjust to the darkness and then twisted the top from her drink. She remembered the old movies where merely looking into the vampire's eyes would drag an innocent victim under his spell.

The memory of losing her train of thought while staring into Viktor's eyes intruded into her ruminations. She'd probably imagined that. Too little sleep. The whole setting had likely fueled her imagination, making her feel things that weren't real.

She would be the first to confess she at times over-reacted to anything related to the paranormal. It wasn't that she didn't have an open mind, but she simply refused to believe.

Viktor Azariel needed a top-of-the-line shrink and a long, Caribbean vacation to get some color back into his pale skin.

She moved to the parlor, where her home computer and desk occupied one corner and provided her an office away from the office. Her grandmother wouldn't care for the addition to her roomful of charming antiques and framed samplers, but that couldn't be helped.

Rowen groped along the wall for the switch. Just as her fingers latched on to it, the whisper of a breath filtered across her shoulder.

Rowen swiveled on her heel…peered through the darkness, her Glock leveled for firing at anything that moved. She held her breath…listened. The muffled sound of the wind rattling the windows…and nothing.

But she'd sensed…felt…something.

"Who's there?"

If it was Hunter again, this time she would shoot.

She listened above the thud of her own pounding heart and heard nothing. After another minute or two of silence, she decided she'd only imagined the sensation.

"Idiot," she muttered.

Rowen lowered her weapon and flipped the light switch.

She stamped across the room to her desk and sat down, plopped her gun on the right side of her computer and her drink on the left. She hated when she got creeped out like this. Apparently being a grown woman made no difference. She was still a fraidy cat. Afraid of dying, afraid of the dark, though she forced herself to live with the latter.

Her fingers lit on the keyboard. She pulled up her work files and got to it. She had to do this part on her own. The chief didn't want anyone else in on this aspect. She hated leaving Merv out, but she understood the chief's concerns. There had already been one leak and as sure as she was that Merv hadn't had anything to do with it, she had her orders.

She sat there for hours. Read until her vision blurred and her shoulders ached from slumping over the computer. She took the last sip of her drink and propped her arm on her desk so she could rest her head comfortably against it. Anything to lessen the tension on her neck.

Just a little longer and she would drag herself back upstairs to bed for a couple more hours of sleep.

"*Rowen.*"

He whispered her name against her skin. She felt the goose bumps rise in reaction to his lips tasting that sensitive flesh near her earlobe.

"You are so beautiful."

She trembled as his mouth trailed along the line of her jaw, the words vibrating softly.

Then he kissed her cheek. "Sleep well."

Rowen wanted to whisper back, her body ached for him. But she was so tired. She couldn't open her eyes…couldn't move her head. She just wanted to sleep and keep dreaming about this delicious dark, alluring man who tempted her dreams far too often.

A LOW GROWL prodded Rowen, but she refused to open her eyes.

Not yet. Please, not yet.

The growl grew louder and something else…another sound…

Rowen knew she had to wake up, but the lure of sleep was just too sweet, too seductive.

Another rumbling growl.

"Ouch!"

Rowen's eyes fluttered open.

What the hell? She jerked her hand upward. Rubbed her fingers together.

Princess yapped.

Rowen cleared the sleep from her eyes, only then realizing she'd conked out at her computer. Princess had tried to wake her by growling and nipping at her fingers. Rowen flexed her fingers and shook her arms to rid them of the prickly sensations. She'd slept with one dangling downward and the other under her head.

The telephone rang and she jumped, startled.

Her machine picked up and she realized then that the ringing phone had been the other sound that had dragged her from the depths of slumber deeper than any she'd had in weeks. It took four rings to turn on the machine.

Rowen scrubbed a hand over her face and reached for the receiver to catch the call.

Something stopped her midreach.

She stared down at herself.

The crocheted throw that usually draped the back of her sofa, the one tattered from use since it was her favorite, hung around her, except, of course, where she'd shaken her arms and caused it to slip down around the chair.

She looked at the couch, then back at the throw her grandmother had made decades ago.

How the hell?

Then she remembered the whispered words…the kiss. Her pulse tripped into a faster rhythm and her fingers went instantly to the spot.

She'd dreamed of him kissing her…whispering passionately to her.

Reason insisted that she had probably gotten up in the night and pulled the throw around her and she just didn't remember doing it.

There had to be a logical explanation.

There always was. Or maybe she simply refused to acknowledge anything else.

The sound of her partner's voice speaking into the answering machine suddenly cut through the worrisome thoughts.

"We've got another body, Ro. Meet me at…"

The rest registered vaguely, but Rowen had stopped listening after his first words.

They had another body.

Chapter Five

Rowen stood on the sidewalk outside the small coffee shop and bakery at the corner of Clarendon and Tremont streets. The morning was crisp and clear. Clean from the night's steady rain. She surveyed the three-hundred-sixty-degree view of cozy cafés and eateries, bookstores and the Boston Center for the Arts Theatre. Chic shops accompanied by upscale luxury housing.

A far cry from the place where Carlotta Simpson had lost her life.

Rowen badged her way past the uniforms stationed at the bakery's entrance. Inside, the sugary sweet scents of Danish and cinnamon rolls still permeated the air from yesterday's baking. But the glass display cases sat empty, like jewel boxes that had been plundered by a thief. Fresh brewed coffee, its aroma rich and bold, underscored the appetizing smells, making Rowen's stomach rumble. Once again, she'd left home without taking the time to have coffee.

That was becoming a bad habit.

The owner of the bakery, along with two female employees from the morning shift, huddled around a small table in the center of the shop. Merv and Lenny had already conducted initial interviews, so there was no real worry about collusion at this point. The employees, as well as their boss, looked shell-shocked. Walking in to find the evening shift manager dead on the bathroom floor was the last thing any of these three had expected to discover this morning.

Three forensic techs were doing what they did with their nifty gadgets—processing the scene as if it were a puzzle and trying to make the pieces fit. The entire shop would be considered a part of the crime scene. Photos would be taken from multiple angles. Prints would be lifted from every surface. All doors and windows would be checked for tool marks and other signs of forced entry. Hypotheses would be formed as to the method of entry, as well as the perp's manner of overpowering the victim.

"Hey, Ro."

Rowen moved toward the far side of the shop where her partner stood by the door marked Employees Only. He looked a little rumpled, but far more alert than she felt. God, that coffee smelled good, but it would have to wait. She had to get a handle on her middle-of-the-night wanderings that left her without enough sleep and too far away from bed to hear the alarm clock.

"Lenny's talking to the neighboring businesses," Merv said, bringing her up to speed.

Rowen nodded. "Where's the body?"

Merv jerked his head toward the door next to him. "In here."

He led the way into the kitchen. Flour was scattered about on the counters. A huge ball of forgotten dough sat rising amid the white dust. A mixer, its paddles caked with the same dough, sat nearby. Obviously preparations had gotten well underway for the day's business before the body had been discovered.

"They found her in the bathroom about six this morning," Merv told her as they neared the rear of the kitchen. A walk-in cooler, storage room and bathroom took up the remaining square footage of the building.

"The owner had no idea she hadn't closed up and gone home as usual," Merv went on. "The victim lives alone, so no one missed her last night." Rowen's partner hesitated at the door labeled Toilet. "When the owner arrived this morning the lights were out. Doors locked." He shrugged. "He had no clue anything was amiss until Edna, the older of the two female employees, went to the bathroom."

"Nothing missing? Her purse? Bank deposits?"

"Her purse's still in the closet they use for coats and sweaters. Right where she left it. Yesterday's entire take was still in the register. Apparently she never got around to tallying the till."

Well, that sure as hell ruled out robbery. But then, Rowen hadn't really expected anything different.

She slipped on shoe covers, then tugged on a pair of

latex gloves. Her stomach immediately roiled in protest. "Same puncture wounds as the others?"

Merv nodded. "Looks like she's been dead for most of the night. Rig's already set in."

Fury swept through Rowen, obliterating the nausea. They had to find this bastard. Or group of bastards. There could be more than one killer. A cult, maybe related to someone exactly like Viktor Azariel.

She forced away the anger, resurrected some semblance of her objectivity. She had to find a neutral place before looking at the body. Focus.

Rowen glanced at her watch. It was just after eight now; that would make her partner's rudimentary assessment of time of death about right. The shop closed at seven on weeknights. With no one around to witness the gruesome act, the victim had likely met her demise shortly after that.

"Cost on his way?" Rowen was actually surprised the M.E. hadn't beaten her here.

"Yep."

"Didn't find anything else?" She glanced around the near spotless kitchen, already knowing the answer but asking just the same. Other than the baking preparations, the place was immaculate. Neat, orderly, not a single can, bag, wooden spoon or whisk out of place.

"Nope. Not yet."

When she reached for the door, Merv made her hesitate. "This one…" He cleared his throat. "This one's different, Ro."

Apprehension inched up her back. Rowen searched her partner's face for some indication of just how different he meant. "Different how?"

He blinked, but in that fraction of a second before his lids dropped over his eyes she saw the flash of horror in his gaze.

"I think you need to see for yourself."

Bracing for the worst, and suddenly finding herself inexplicably breathless, Rowen took a much needed breath and opened the door to the bathroom.

Instantly the odor of coagulated blood assaulted her nostrils. She resisted the impulse to gag. The more appealing aroma of sugary baked goods, in conjunction with the exhaust fan, had effectively camouflaged the clawing scent of death until the door had been opened.

The room wasn't very large, perhaps eight feet by eight feet. A white toilet with a scarred blue seat and a wallmounted porcelain washbowl were the only fixtures. A metal cabinet stood against one wall and likely housed supplies, toilet paper and the like. The floor was tiled in black-and-white squares, not the stone or ceramic kind, but the less expensive stick-on vinyl sort. The walls had been painted a clean white, but over time the color had aged to a faint yellow.

As soon as she'd allowed the details of the bigger picture to penetrate her senses, Rowen focused on the condition and position of the victim.

The air evacuated her lungs all over again.

"Her name's Ellen Green. Twenty-five," Merv said. "Single."

Her partner was right. This one was way different. And now she understood why he'd waited for her to see this for herself before he offered details.

The pale white skin of Miss Green's throat was marred by two small puncture wounds, just like the other victims. The major, glaring difference in her death was the blood. It appeared that every drop of the life-giving fluid, rather than being drained and carried from the scene, had been allowed to pool on the glossy black-and-white tiles beneath her body.

"Oh, God." Rowen crouched down to make a closer inspection, being careful not to tread on or even near any of the evidence.

The victim's face was frozen in that same death mask as the others, as if she'd glimpsed pure terror before dying. Her arms hung loosely, giving the impression that she'd simply sat down and welcomed her coming fate. Her legs were tucked modestly to one side. She wore her beige button-up uniform dress, name tag and pin designating her as part of management and the requisite slip-resistant shoes. Her hair was still restrained in traditional food-handler style.

Rowen wondered if the current employees would ever be able to walk into this room again and not see Ellen Green sitting on the floor in a crimson circle of her own blood. The stench would linger, no matter what the cleaning efforts, like a bad memory. The resonance

of one final scream would reverberate each time anyone who had witnessed the results of this brutal act entered the small room and recalled the violence.

When Rowen had seen enough, she stepped back. Dr.
Cost had arrived by then. This time, he'd brought along
his assistant so Rowen stayed out of the way. Trying to
crowd into the small room would exacerbate the risk of
contaminating evidence.

"I could use some coffee," Merv said abruptly, dragging Rowen's attention back to him. "How 'bout you,
Ro? You had any this morning?"

She exhaled a weary sigh. "I could use a cup." Despite the way her stomach churned just now, she desperately needed the caffeine. This was going to be a
long day.

And it was only going to get worse.

By the time she'd managed to force down the coffee,
Cost had stepped from the bathroom and ordered the
body taken away on a gurney. His assistant oversaw the
body's removal. But when the attendants were about to
leave with the victim carefully enveloped in a trace
sheet and body bag, Cost stopped their progress.

He motioned for Rowen to join him next to the gurney. "Take a look at this," he murmured for her ears only.
He unzipped the bag and pulled back the sheet far
enough to reveal the victim's upper torso. Using a
freshly gloved hand, he parted her bloodstained dress
where it buttoned over her chest. On her right breast was
a small tattoo featuring a dogwood blossom.

Rowen's heart stumbled. "Is it the same?"

He nodded to his assistant, who instantly produced a handheld magnifying glass. Rowen took the tool and peered at the tattoo and immediately distinguished the letters…the word.

Donor.

"Now," Cost said quietly, "we have a connection between two of the victims besides the cause of death. All you have to do, Detective, is figure out what the hell it means."

By NOON, the M.E. had given the chief a verbal preliminary report on the latest victim. And considering the theories all the newspapers, as well as the local broadcast news media were tossing around, mostly revolving around the *V* word, the case got upgraded.

Rowen glanced around the Boston PD conference room. Chief Koppel had assigned an additional detective to their little task force, bringing the count to four. Along with her partner, Merv Gant, and fellow detective Lenny Doherty, was a newbie who'd just transferred over from Robbery, Jeff Finch. Finch had passed his detective's exam just six months ago and was champing at the bit to sink his teeth into what he called a real case.

Rowen resisted the urge to say, *Well, here's your chance.*

Unfortunately, the cops weren't in the conference room alone.

"Detectives," the chief announced, "this is Dr. Smith Forrester. He's a criminal psychologist and the university was kind enough to lend him to us this morning. Dr. Forrester has reviewed the file and I've brought him up to speed on our latest discoveries." As the chief said the last his gaze settled briefly on Rowen. "So, heads up, detectives. We need all the help we get here."

Forrester wasn't the shrink Homicide generally used, leading Rowen to believe this one was more specialized, but the chief didn't bother explaining.

Since the rest of the detectives did not know about the dogwood blossom, the chief suggested Rowen fill everyone in. She didn't miss the question in her partner's eyes. She would have to make this right with him. In the years they had worked together, she had never once hidden anything from him.

In many respects Rowen and Merv were a pretty good fit. Though Merv was more than twenty years older and had been married for nearly as long as Rowen had been alive, he had the heart of a much younger man. He was the perfect partner. Never made a fuss and didn't have an ego problem.

She hoped that wasn't about to change with this morning's meeting.

Nearly an hour later, the good doctor, who appeared to have tired of hearing himself talk generalities, finally got down to the nitty-gritty.

"I agree with your conclusion that you're dealing

with a cult of sorts," he announced as if his permission had been essential.

Images of Viktor Azariel kept flashing in Rowen's mind. She thought of last night's dreams and shivered. That was definitely the first time she'd dreamed of a suspect, at least in that way.

"Clearly this is the work of more than one person. With the lack of resistance on the part of the victims, it's most likely someone the victim knows."

So far, so good. Considering Viktor Azariel's connection to Carlotta Simpson, that made him a prime suspect. Rowen had already decided that before the doc had said as much.

"I don't believe this act has any sexual undertones, nor do I feel the unknown subject is trying to prove self-worth or any other personal validation. These killings have been carried out at very precise times and locations. No witnesses, no evidence left behind. This alone takes very careful planning, as I am sure you all know."

Rowen shifted in her seat, tried to pay attention to the speaker, but the passion in Viktor Azariel's voice kept echoing in her ears. Carlotta Simpson had been one of his. If the latest victim was also, as Rowen suspected, Azariel might turn vigilante.

There was always the possibility that this latest donor belonged to someone else…like Azariel. Rowen absolutely refused to use the *V* word. Maybe this one, Ellen Green, was a revenge kill. After all, there was that one significant difference. Wasting her blood seemed to be a challenge, a message of some sort. For whom? Azariel?

Forrester was saying, "Killers hunt in their comfort zone, ladies and gentlemen. All of them. They have their territory. I'm certain you've already triangulated the area, based on the discovery of the bodies. But we'll need far more than that to catch this wily killer. Since we have nothing on the unknown subject, we should turn our focus to the victims."

Rowen mentally reviewed the list of victims. Four women, one man. All young, healthy. Only two marked as donors.

"Who were these victims?" Forrester went on. "Why were they chosen? Most predators attack the weakest among society. That isn't consistent with the victims in this case. One victim was a man, young, strong. The others were women, also young. All were educated, thriving individuals. Did they belong to a cult of any sort? What motivation did they have for giving in to death so easily? I believe this is your best avenue at this juncture."

And then the good doctor said something that made complete and simple sense to Rowen.

"Dig deeper, detectives. No one dies for naught. There will be motivation. Look close enough and you will find it. As for method, I agree with your M.E. The blood was drained from the victim while he or she still breathed. Think about it." He shrugged nonchalantly. "A pumping heart would make the process far easier."

Rowen blinked, felt her skin tingle where she'd imagined that breath had whispered across it last night.

"Excuse me, Dr. Forrester," Rowen interrupted whatever he'd intended to say next. "Why the wasted blood with this latest victim? If this is the work of a cult, it seems the blood would have been gathered for some purpose. Ritual sacrifice, self-healing. Whatever. Why go to the trouble to kill someone and then leave the bounty on the floor?" She needed to know if his conclusions would be the same as hers.

"Excellent point, Detective O'Connor. If we go with the theory that this is the work of a cult that uses the blood for a specific purpose, then the latest victim was either a mistake, which I doubt, or a message."

"The scene was every bit as clean as the others." She gave a small shrug. "I suppose it's possible someone that methodical made a mistake in the final step." Not right, she decided. "But why let it *all* go to waste? Why not save what he could? Whatever the method being used, surely it could have been stopped or adjusted."

"Another valid point," the doctor agreed. "However, our killer or killers are all too human to fall outside the realm of mistakes. Things could simply have gone wrong, but I would lean more toward the idea that this was a message for someone."

Rowen gave herself a pat on the back for that one.

Merv spoke up then. "You're saying our killer wanted to prove something to someone?"

"Yes," Forrester confirmed. "But this is purely speculation. What we need are more details. Find out who the victims were and you'll learn certain truths about your suspect."

Rowen decided his suggestion was by far the straightest avenue for this going-nowhere investigation.

As the meeting broke up, Merv sidled up to her. "Can we have our own conference?"

"Sure." Now was as good a time as any to clear the air, she supposed.

Since privacy was a premium anywhere in the division, she followed her partner into the coffee room. He closed the door, a move that might buy them a few minutes.

"What's the deal with the tattoo?"

God, she hated that the chief had suckered her into this.

"The chief asked me to keep it quiet for a few days. Look into it off the record, so to speak."

Merv grunted. "Well, when you're following orders, you're following orders."

The ease with which he accepted her excuse for shutting him out made Rowen feel even guiltier. But, as he'd said, she was only following orders.

"Thanks, Merv, for giving me a break on this. You know I would never leave you out of the loop unless I had no choice." And that was the truth.

"So, what do you make of Forrester?" Merv poured himself a cup of coffee and took advantage of the privacy they somehow managed to maintain beyond ninety seconds. Considering the three coffeepots in this lounge were the only ones on the floor, that was a record.

Rowen thought about that for a time. "I think he's right." But then, it was an elementary leap. Since robbery and sexual assault had been ruled out, that left only two possibilities: random selection of victims or personal vendetta. "We need to learn all we can about the vics and see where it takes us."

"All four of us?"

It wasn't until he asked the question that she realized how her suggestion sounded. Bodies were piling up; they needed to divide and conquer.

"Of course not." What was wrong with her lately? She couldn't keep blaming her missteps on lack of sleep. Hunter's dark image immediately formed in her head. Maybe it was him. His reappearance had shaken her more than she wanted to admit. She had to get past it.

"Put Lenny and the new guy, Finch, on the first three victims, but I want you focused on these last two, Simpson and Green."

"Any particular reason you want me on the last two, other than the tattoo?"

Dammit. He knew she was still keeping something from him. But she just wasn't ready to talk about Viktor Azariel. She told herself it had nothing to do with protecting him on some totally insane level. But it felt exactly like that.

"You think maybe we're looking at different killers here?" her partner prodded.

That was always a possibility, but that wasn't her thinking. "Maybe Forrester's right, maybe this last one was a message to someone. And since both the last two vics had the same tattoo, let's assume maybe they were both warnings." *She was mine.* Viktor's words echoed again.

Before Merv could ask, she said, "I'm going to delve into the cults practicing in the area. If I need backup, I'll let you know."

His gaze narrowed suspiciously, but he kept those suspicions to himself. "Just be careful, Ro."

She gifted him with the smile he expected. "I'm always careful, Merv, you know that."

EVAN WAITED in the deepest shadows of the parking garage until Rowen returned to her vehicle.

She insisted on continuing to participate in this investigation despite his warnings. That didn't surprise him, but it did concern him greatly.

His assessment wasn't complete by any means, but he had his reservations as to where this was headed.

Someone had started a war in the seething dark side of this city. More people would die before it was over.

Pain seared through his brain with the troubling thoughts and Rowen's connection to them. He closed his eyes and waited for it to pass. Only a few days, and already his tolerance to the medication was building.

Time was even shorter than he had realized.

He moved along the murky edges of darkness, keeping close to the wall and watching as she unlocked her vehicle by keyless remote when she neared it. Even now, after his warning, her defenses were not fully in place. How could he make her see the danger?

When she reached to open the driver's door, he came up behind her and put his hand on her arm. "*Rowen,* we need to talk."

She spun around, leveled the barrel of her weapon in his face before he could back off. "You shouldn't sneak up on me like that, Hunter. You could end up as dead as I thought you were all these years."

Though she attempted to pass off the bitterness in her voice as sarcasm, he saw through her. He'd hurt her; there would be no altering that cold, hard fact.

"You have another body," he said, getting straight to the point. "The killing won't stop, *Rowen.* Your life is in danger. You must listen to me—"

She lowered the weapon, but she took her time doing so. "Have you been following me?" She inclined her head and studied him. His heart rate reacted, stirring the remnants of pain that never really went away. Not in three long years. "Stalking is against the law, in case you didn't know. Doesn't the FBI teach little things like that at the Farm?"

He wanted to shake her, but that tactic would only worsen her unforgiving attitude. "Do not trust Viktor Azariel." He sensed that was where she was leaning in her investigation. Viktor was his prime suspect, as well, but for different reasons. Reasons Rowen did not need to know.

Shoving the Glock back into the shoulder holster she

wore beneath her jacket, she looked directly at him and let him have it. This time, the sarcasm was real. "You know, Hunter, you really should loosen up. I'm a big girl. I can take care of myself."

She reached behind her and opened the door, then used it as a barrier between them. "Not to mention," she added with that cocky self-confidence he'd always admired, "I have a big gun and I know how to use it."

Rowen cut him a warning look. "Keep that in mind next time you break into my house or sneak up on me."

She ducked into the car, slid behind the wheel.

"You should get more sleep, *Rowen,*" he said quietly, knowing she would understand that the comment entailed more than advice for her future reference. "You're more vulnerable than you know."

Any tolerant feelings she still possessed vanished with the next beat of her heart. He watched her expression darken with anger. "Stay away from me, Hunter. I'm finished playing this game with you. Your hurt me once. I won't let you close enough to do it again."

He grabbed the door before she could slam it shut. "I am not the enemy, *Rowen.* Know that if you know nothing else."

"Step away from the vehicle," she ordered.

"Stay away from Viktor. He's not who you think he is," Evan pressed for all the good it would do. He released the door and stepped back.

She slammed the door, rocketed into reverse and out of the parking slot, cut her wheels sharply, jammed the gearshift into Drive and sped away without sparing him another glance.

There was only one place she could go for answers. Straight into the lair of his most lethal enemy.

Chapter Six

Rage boiled inside Rowen during the entire trip to the Berkshires.

Evan Hunter had no business coming back into her life now or ever.

Why the hell had he come back after all this time?

She cut into the left lane and went around the idiot determined to drive fifty miles per hour in a zone authorizing a higher speed.

She never got like this. Never lost her temper so easily. She banged her fist against the steering wheel. It was him. And this damned case.

Rowen forced herself to relax against the headrest, loosened her death grip on the steering wheel. This whole damned case was insane.

There were no such things as vampires. Sure, there were those who'd talked themselves into believing they weren't like other humans. It was an escape tactic as old as time. Pretend to be something else when you hated who you really were. Teenagers did it every day.

Unfortunately for the rest of society, some poor souls outgrew adolescence and went straight into personality disorder.

It didn't take a degree in psychology, no offense to Dr. Forrester, to know that's what was happening here. Deviants were killing people for their blood. It wasn't as if bizarre occurrences didn't happen from time to time. In Homicide, she'd seen it all. But this was a whole other shooting match.

This killer had technique—clean, precise, almost clinical.

How the hell did he get the victims to sit quietly as he drained away their life?

She'd obsessed on that little detail for the past forty-eight hours. Sure, there were people in this world who wanted to be needed so badly that they sacrificed way more than they should, but this went so far beyond that that it hit another stratosphere. No one in his right mind would permit such a thing.

Unless he or she were a fanatic.

Rowen heaved out a sigh.

Dr. Forrester had urged that they learn all they could about the victims to help solve the case. Well, Rowen knew one fact for certain. These were young, healthy, strong, intelligent people with bright futures and the expectancy of long lives ahead of them.

Suicide didn't make sense, and suicide was exactly what the scene staging suggested.

Staging.

The epiphany struck abruptly and with gut-wrenching force. Each victim had looked as if he or she had merely sat down or fallen without putting up any sort of resistance to his or her attacker.

That's the way the perp wanted it to look.

It was so clear now.

Why hadn't she seen that before?

Her earlier hunch was right on target. Just before she'd left the office, she'd called Dr. Cost and sent him on a search for the proverbial needle in a haystack.

Look for the most obscure drug you know, she'd urged, anything that leaves no typical residue in the human system, and which causes instant paralysis.

That would explain a hell of a lot.

If Dr. Cost could isolate the right drug, which might not show up in routine tox screens, and then find the way it was introduced into the victim…

Big, fat, major *if.*

For now, she had another avenue to pursue. At least two of the victims had been "donors"; she needed to understand exactly what that term meant, what the commitment entailed. If Viktor Azariel was acquainted with both Simpson and Green, Rowen needed to know whatever he knew. If she had to arrest him and drag him in as an individual of interest to the case, by God, she would. The chief might have a stroke if she did that. He wanted the Azariel connection kept quiet for now. He wanted her alone following up on the eccentric man.

The idea that Azariel's major financial interest was vested in a pharmaceuticals company hadn't escaped her, either. His minions could have developed just the kind of drug that would instantly paralyze a victim and prove undetectable in routine screenings.

She turned onto the long, winding drive that led to his property. The guard glanced at her ID and motioned her through the gate. One glance in her rearview mirror told her the guard had just called her in.

Mr. Azariel would know she was coming before she parked in front of his massive granite steps.

The butler, or whatever the older gentleman in the nice suit was supposed to be, waited on the steps just like before. Rowen climbed out of her car and walked straight toward him without hesitation.

"I apologize for any inconvenience, Detective O'Connor," he offered politely but firmly. "However, you've arrived at an inopportune time and Mr. Azariel isn't available for visitors."

She glanced at her watch. Just past three in the afternoon. How inopportune could her timing be? Too early for bed, a little late for lunch.

"As you say I've come a long way and I—"

"Mr. Azariel is not taking visitors," he repeated. This time, the politeness was absent.

Now that pissed her off. "I tell you what." She climbed the final two steps that separated them, then flashed her creds. "This is official business, not a social call. Now, you let Mr. Azariel know I'm here to see him.

If he chooses not to see me, then we'll have to take the meeting to One Schroeder Plaza."

The guy was good, his stoic expression stayed exactly the same. "You may wait in the foyer." He executed a sharp about-face and led the way into the house.

The stark contrast from outside to inside struck her all over again. Mr. Azariel needed a new decorator.

"Wait here," the servant reiterated once the massive bronze doors closed behind her.

She nodded and continued her study of the primitive architecture as the man hurried to give his employer the bad news. The cop wasn't going away.

Rowen walked around the mammoth hall and surveyed the artwork. She hadn't had time to pay much attention to smaller details on her last visit. Too many other elements had been vying for her attention.

The final piece at the darkest end of the corridor was Viktor Azariel himself captured on canvas. No mistake about that. She couldn't guess when the portrait had been done, but it looked old. And yet, the lord of the manor appeared exactly as he did today.

Okay, hadn't she watched this scene in a movie? Next, he would tell her how many hundred years old he was.

Not going there.

She shivered as the dank chill settled into her bones. Like a cave. The place even smelled old. Then she remembered that it was. Centuries old. How could she have forgotten reading about the enormous castle-moving project?

"Detective?"

Rowen turned around. "Yes?"

The butler stood at the bottom of the ominous staircase that led up to the second floor. Grotesquely disfigured heads had been intricately carved into the spindles. A wolf's head, its mouth open and baring fangs, topped the newel post. "Mr. Azariel says that you may come up."

That gave her pause. "Up? Up where?"

"He's waiting for you in his suite."

A trickle of fear made its presence known deep in her chest. No need to be afraid; she was still in charge of this situation. "I think the parlor would be more appropriate." She gestured to the door which led to the room where they'd first talked.

The gentleman didn't bother responding. He had his orders. Rowen knew that feeling.

Well, she'd demanded a meeting. She supposed allowing Mr. Azariel to select the part of his home in which he would take the meeting was the least she could do.

She followed his hired help up the garishly embellished staircase and slid her hand along the polished banister the same way she did at home. The sound of their steps echoed in the massive space, bounced off the barren walls.

How did anyone live like this? With no real creature comforts?

Upstairs proved no more suitable.

Dark…cold…forbidding. A long corridor split the space in half—east and west wings, maybe. At the far end of the corridor to the right stood two enormous doors.

When her escort stopped outside those looming double doors, an odd moment of déjà vu made Rowen sway slightly. Too weird.

She shook it off and steeled herself for whatever she would encounter as the doors were drawn open.

Dragging in a deep breath, she entered the room. The doors immediately closed behind her.

Viktor Azariel lounged on a sofa near the room's fireplace, which resembled the one in the parlor downstairs. Two chairs and a table were the only other furnishings. Her host's penetrating gaze immediately settled on her with the same suffocating heaviness she felt with each breath she took in his home.

"I appreciate your seeing me, Mr. Azariel," she said when she'd found her voice. He remained silent.

Without speaking, he stood and strode toward her.

Rowen recognized the tactic for what it was—intimidation. She told herself to focus, to pay attention. She'd been trained to do that in any situation, under the worst conditions. But the details registered slowly. She couldn't quite understand how or why he had that effect on her, but she'd noticed it before. Today, his hair hung long, draped against his shoulders…bare shoulders. No shirt. Black trousers, like before. Her gaze scooted back up to his chest. She told herself to look away, but somehow she couldn't.

His skin looked pale and smooth…stretched tightly over well-developed muscles. For one second, the urge to reach out and touch him—to see if he felt as cold and unreachable as he looked—was almost overwhelming.

"Detective," he said in that deep, deep voice. "What brings you to see me today?"

Rowen tried to read his eyes, but he didn't allow her to see beyond the rich, dark color that made her feel unreasonably ill at ease.

"I have more questions for you." Her voice wasn't quite as steady as she'd hoped for, but it was the best she could do. Hunter's warning ricocheted through her head, but she forced it away.

"Yes," he said before she'd asked the first one, "Ellen Green was mine." Something primal flickered in his eyes. "She's dead, no?"

Rowen swallowed to dampen her throat. She really hated the idea that he could apparently read her mind. But then, why else would she be here, right? The thought gave her some comfort.

"I'd like you to explain this donor system to me."

His gaze did a thorough exploration of her body, coming to rest on the area where her Glock rested in her shoulder holster. Her pulse reacted.

"Am I a suspect, Detective?"

What was the point in lying? "Yes."

He smiled, drawing her attention to his mouth. The cut and fullness of it made her chest feel tight.

Breathe. Concentrate. Don't get lost in the details, Rowen. Observe and evaluate.

"I suppose I shouldn't be surprised. Why else would you have come back?"

Rowen ignored the question. "The more we learn

about the victims, the closer we'll get to the killer," she offered, recapping the psychologist's words. "We need to follow up on anyone connected to their lives. You, by your own admission, have a connection."

Azariel nodded. "I see." He stroked his smooth chin. "You're looking for motive."

Irritation overrode the other confusing emotions this man evoked in her. How could he act so nonchalantly? "Five people are dead, sir. I'm looking for justice."

"Of course you are," he agreed, his tone barely a cut above condescending. "It would be a disgrace for anyone to die for naught."

Now he was paraphrasing the psychologist's words. How the hell did he do that? "Don't patronize me, Mr. Azariel," she said curtly, maybe more so than she should have.

His expression turned hard instantly. "I would never patronize you, *Rowen.*"

The way he said her name—exactly as Hunter did—rattled her, made her think of shadowy dreams and restless nights.

Another set of doors on the other side of the room suddenly opened. These likely led to where he slept. Rowen's gaze jerked in that direction, her attention piqued in anticipation of what she might see. The idea of a coffin flitted briefly through her head. She mentally kicked herself for momentarily going stupid.

A woman, obviously nude and wrapped in a sheet,

appeared in the open doorway. Her blond hair fell all the way to her hips. Even from across the room Rowen saw the small tattoo on her right shoulder.

"Viktor, are you coming back to bed?" she asked coyly.

Rowen looked away. She could feel her face turning red with the heat of embarrassment. The reality of what she'd interrupted shouldn't have bothered her. She'd caught suspects in far more compromising positions. Her reaction screamed of a lack of objectivity. She had to get a handle on her screwed-up emotions.

This was Hunter's fault.

She gritted her teeth and forced her attention back to the matter at hand. He had put her off balance and she just couldn't seem to get it back.

The impatient blonde tossed her head and that mane of thick hair twirled over her shoulders to cascade down her back. The move revealed her neck more fully and Rowen's breath stalled in the vicinity of her seizing lungs. Two small puncture wounds marred the creamy perfection of her slender throat.

Rowen blinked, noted somewhere in her peripheral vision that Viktor made a vague sort of gesture with the fingers of one hand.

Images of him and this woman making love flashed one after the other, splintering her attention. When she cleared her mind and looked again, the woman had retreated back into what was, as Rowen suspected, the lord's bedroom beyond those double doors.

"You don't want to believe," he said, drawing Rowen's gaze back to his. "You resist that which you don't understand."

She would not be seduced by his words. "I understand murder perfectly, Mr. Azariel. And that's what we're talking about."

"It scares me, as well," he admitted, "at times. But it's there…lurking just around the corner."

She didn't move, didn't speak for fear that he would stop talking now that he'd begun. The distinct impression that they were no longer talking specifically about murder sent off a warning inside her.

"The hunger rages through my blood, pulses just beneath my skin. A force of nature I cannot hope to defeat." His hand flattened on that sculpted chest as he spoke and moved ever nearer to her.

Rowen refused to back away, refused to let him see that she feared him in any way.

"As much as I despise my need—and I do despise it—it fulfills me in a way that nothing else can," he said softly. "Grants a vividness like no other living soul can fathom. Sings to me, promising power and pleasure. And I cannot resist its melody."

He towered over her, showed her the truth of his words with his eyes, and she was mesmerized.

"As beautiful and healing as that need is," he continued in that deep, sensual voice, "when ignored, the pain is equally intense. There is no cure…no hope beyond what I cannot resist…what I know I must do."

"Drink the blood of your victims," she murmured, comprehension clarifying the moment for her.

"It is my curse."

Focus on the case. No feeling sorry for the man who could be a killer.

"So rather than kill to provide for your needs, you have a group of donors who willingly supply your…necessary…requirements."

He knew what she meant.

"That is correct."

His words were slow to penetrate, delaying her responses. Whatever he said, she couldn't seem to take her eyes off his. She tried to reclaim control, but it wasn't happening. Her palms had started to sweat. Her pulse raced with the fear building inside her. This was too crazy. It couldn't be real.

"The relationship is handled discreetly, I presume?" At least she sounded reasonably calm.

"Yes. They come to me at their scheduled times."

Rowen cleared her throat. "How do you…?" She wrestled with the best way to introduce this question. With him standing so close, peering down at her, it was difficult to focus. The woman who'd appeared at the door moments ago kept intruding into her thoughts.

"There are a number of methods," he said in response to her incomplete question. "Removal in the usual manner one would utilize when donating blood. Or…"

Her gaze momentarily dropped to his mouth, but quickly moved back up to his eyes. She wanted to be looking directly at him when he gave this answer, however difficult that might prove to be. "Or?" she prompted.

"I can take it the old-fashioned way, while making love to the donor." He flashed a smile that made her gasp. "Would you like a demonstration, Detective?"

Rowen couldn't breathe. "I…" She struggled to draw in air, but it simply wouldn't pass through her throat, as if something blocked it. She couldn't have seen what she thought she saw…no. This man had made himself what he was. Fiction. Fantasy. Not real.

He moved even closer, leaned down to whisper against her hair. One hand closed around her waist, sending a frightening yearning through her. "Why would I kill them, Detective? They were part of my harvest. I would never waste a human life when it is that very living thing that ultimately gives me life."

No matter what the chief said she should not have come back here alone. Rowen didn't remember how she got out of his room or the house so quickly. One moment, she was staring into those alluring eyes; the next, she was outside in the dark.

She blinked, gasped for air.

Wait…she turned all the way around, stared up at the sky.

It couldn't be dark yet. How could she have been here for hours?

She groped her way around her car and flung herself behind the wheel. She had to get out of here.

She drove straight home. One glance at her cell phone told her she'd missed three calls from her partner. She listened to the voice mails he'd left. The first gave her an update on where he was with his part of the investigation. Both the second and third were just attempts to touch base with her. She couldn't call him back, not right now. He would hear the uncertainty...the downright fear in her voice.

Even after she'd arrived home and struggled to fall into her usual routine of walking Princess, she constantly watched over her shoulder. Felt that persistent presence shadowing her. The reality of those lost hours plowed into her thoughts again. She shuddered. How could it be this late?

She'd lost at least three hours.

How had Azariel done that?

Drugs?

Impossible. She hadn't had anything to drink or eat while she was there.

Hypnosis?

Maybe.

She didn't know.

She hurried Princess through her walk, then locked up the house for the night, taking care to check each window and door at least twice.

For the first time in three years, she longed for the shelter of Hunter's arms. For the comfort she knew he could give her.

Cursing herself every step of the way, Rowen climbed the stairs and ran a hot bath.

Maybe if she relaxed her muscles, she would sleep halfway decent tonight. God knew she needed to recharge her lagging brain cells.

Scrounging up her favorite gown, a floor-length white, gauzy, Victorian-looking chemise, and a clean pair of panties, she started to undress but hesitated. Maybe she should have a glass of wine to go with her bath. Now that might actually do the trick and ensure some decent shut-eye. Considering how her afternoon had gone, a little mental anesthetizing was definitely in order.

With the tub ready and her nightclothes on a nearby chair, she padded downstairs and poured herself a glass of chardonnay. She downed it and poured another.

If she had trouble concentrating tomorrow morning, it wasn't going to have anything to do with lack of sleep or crazy dreams. Not if she could help it, anyway.

She dragged herself back up the stairs and set her glass on the table next to the big old claw-footed tub, lit a couple of candles for the ambience and stripped off her clothes. Shedding her work garb felt liberating. She placed the Glock on the closed toilet lid.

The water welcomed her, instantly calmed her. She slipped deep into the tub and rested her head against the bath pillow Merv's wife had given her for Christmas. She closed her eyes and sipped her wine.

She blocked all thoughts of the case. Right now, she needed to wind down, to forget about the horrors of the day. Tomorrow morning would be soon enough to think about it all again. Not once in her career had her ability to maintain a sense of professionalism been so elusive.

Slowly, the hot water and the wine did its work. Rowen felt more relaxed than she had in days—weeks maybe.

As hard as she tried to block it, the idea that she'd somehow stayed in Viktor Azariel's home for several unaccounted-for hours bobbed to the surface of her hard-gained state of relaxation.

How was that possible?

A frown furrowed her brow, disrupting her calm. But this was too wacked to pretend it hadn't happened. She had no recollection of anything beyond the short verbal exchange she and Viktor had shared. What had happened after that? How had it happened?

Subliminal hypnosis?

God, she just didn't know.

Eventually her respiration slowed, grew even. She was so tired. Too tired to think anymore. As she slipped toward unconsciousness, pictures reeled past in the private theater of her mind. Making love, not wild and frantic movements, but slow, thorough rises and falls, moans and grinds. She could feel the male weight on top of her, feel masculine lips, full lips, devouring hers. The press of his hard-barreled sex against her making her ache to be filled.

It had been so long…three endless years.

"*Rowen.*"

Hunter's voice.

But the man moving over her was not Hunter.

Viktor…

She tried to wake up…tried to open her eyes but she couldn't. She felt herself climaxing…felt her body contract with that moment of swelling pleasure. He plunged deep inside her one last time and then his mouth opened wider and she saw the unholiest part of him…

Rowen jerked up. Water splashed over the edges of the tub. She gasped frantically for breath.

She coughed. Choked.

She'd fallen asleep and slipped beneath the water's surface.

She sputtered and gasped until she got her breath back.

When she'd stopped wheezing for oxygen, she pulled the drain plug, her hand shaking turbulently, and got out. Shivering from the cool air on her damp skin, she quickly dried off and wrapped a towel around herself. Her limbs felt weak with the receding fear…and the other sensation she didn't want to acknowledge.

She picked up the wineglass that had slipped from her fingers and dropped onto the throw rug, the thick wooly fabric all that had kept it from breaking on the tiled floor.

How had she done something so stupid?

What infuriated her the most was the way her body still throbbed with the fading waves of an orgasm she'd reached in her sleep.

And almost drowned in the process.

Now there was a wet dream she'd just as soon forget.

Chapter Seven

Evan watched her sleep. Careful not to make a sound or any sudden moves, as much for his benefit as for hers. She wasn't going to like what he'd done. But it was the only way to protect her.

He was too weak to risk waiting any longer for her to see things his way.

More and more of the medication was required to give him any measurable resistance to the mind-shattering pain. Soon all his efforts would fail, and he could not take the chance that Rowen would still, at that point, refuse to listen to his warnings.

Viktor, the bastard, had crossed the line. Effectively goading Evan into a desperate move. But then, Evan wasn't surprised. He'd halfway expected as much.

Rowen had, unknowingly, gotten herself trapped in the middle of a war.

Evan understood what was happening here, even if she did not and even if the cast of players had not as yet been identified. Someone had decided to wage a battle against Viktor's kind. Evan was still unclear about the motive. But the end result was crystal clear—many more would die.

The media was the enemy's tool. If the body count continued to rise, unrest and panic would invade the community like a disease of biblical proportions. And while this mass hysteria played out, distracting the authorities, the real war would take place.

Ellen Green had been a blatant message to Viktor Azariel. As one of his donors, the precious commodity that had pulsed in her veins had been poured out, wasted, waved like a red flag. Viktor would seek revenge. But the question was, against whom?

He couldn't know who the enemy was any more than Evan. Or did he?

Evan had reason to believe that his old nemesis wanted him preoccupied while this war played itself out.

It would be dawn soon. With Rowen safe, perhaps he should get the necessary confrontation over with. Time was Evan's enemy. There was none to waste. And though daylight hours proved the most physically draining, his choices were limited.

He pressed a kiss to Rowen's forehead, allowed the sensation to wash over him despite the pain he would endure as a result of it.

With the house he'd chosen as a safe haven securely locked and Rowen still sleeping off the effects of the drug, he drove to the Berkshires.

Azariel's mighty keep wasn't that far away. Evan

had chosen carefully when he'd planned his steps, allowing himself easy access to the one primary player he recognized.

When he parked in the circular drive, Viktor was already waiting for him on the front steps.

"I expected you sooner," he said mockingly.

Evan ignored the remark and followed him inside those massive stone walls. He had no desire to exchange idle chitchat with his nemesis in the open.

Whispered sounds echoed in the hall. Viktor was not alone. He had apparently summoned those closest to him. Evan could feel their presence. The heaviness of it bore down on him, made him feel weak. He dispensed with the pointless waste of energy, refused to bow to the weight of it. This battle was between the two of them. Honor would not allow Viktor to rely on others.

"Would you like some wine?"

Evan pinned him with his gaze. "You know why I came here."

"I'll take that as a no," Viktor said glibly.

"Talk, now, while you still can," Evan threatened, his rage momentarily getting the better of him. "Your continued survival is looking dim at best."

"I have no control over the situation. I know nothing useful to you." Viktor sat down on one of the sofas and gestured to the other. "It is out of my hands."

"You must know who sent the message," Evan pressed relentlessly. It had to be one of Viktor's kind who wanted to destroy him. Someone who wanted to hold his position as a royal.

Viktor shrugged. "I have no idea. But whoever he is, he will die a slow, painful death."

Evan had difficulty believing he had no idea whatsoever about this new enemy. He was far too calm for that. "One of your breed?"

Since Evan had not chosen to sit down, Viktor stood, assuming a more cautious stance. His senses were too guarded. It was quite impossible to judge what he might be hiding.

"Most definitely not," he countered savagely, giving away a mere glimpse of his emotional state.

Evan's suspicions were aroused more fully. He'd obviously hit a sensitive spot. "How can you be so certain? You and yours have been a closely kept secret for decades. Who else could know of your beliefs?"

Another blast of fury lit the other man's eyes. "Decades? Beliefs?" He scoffed. "You still refuse to *believe* the truth that we have existed for centuries." He shook his head. "What a shame, when it is only by virtue of our breed that you're still alive."

His jaw tightening, Evan met that lethal gaze head-on. He would not be distracted by double-talk. "I'm alive because I was lucky." The rage he felt set off a chain reaction in his brain, making him shudder with pain, but he quickly snatched back some measure of control.

"You see," Viktor bemused. "You have the sickness."

Evan resisted the urge to storm across the room and pound the bastard senseless. "You're wrong."

Viktor quirked an eyebrow. "Am I?" He studied Evan for three beats. "You have all the symptoms. A sensitivity to light, touch, sound. Even now, the medication provides little relief. You are this close—" he held his forefinger and thumb within millimeters of each other "—to breaking. You need the healing that only one thing will give."

Evan tamped down his mounting rage. That's what the fool wanted, to keep him off balance. "The damage was caused by the explosion." The same explosion that had killed his entire team…three years ago. He was supposed to have died, as well, but somehow he'd hung on by a thread. But when he'd come out of the coma, he'd been left with side effects from the extensive trauma. All his senses were greatly enhanced, but not in a good way. The slightest vibration of sound pounded against his eardrums causing excruciating pain. Light, natural or artificial, blinded him. He could literally smell a person's fear, hear his heart thumping in his chest, feel the urgency of his every need and desire.

It was a fate worse than death.

"You would not have survived had you not carried a portion of my genetic material…you know that, Hunter, even if you refuse to admit it," Viktor said with much smugness.

"I place no merit on the supernatural," Evan protested. "Not then, not now."

"So foolish." Viktor sighed. "Why did you ever agree

to work with the FBI's paranormal studies unit? Were you the token nonbeliever?"

"We were all nonbelievers," Evan countered. "Our work was quite specific. Find a logical explanation for all so-called psychic phenomena. Just as we did when we discovered your *breed*." He used the term merely because Viktor insisted his followers were a special breed, not quite human. But Evan knew better.

"I allowed you to analyze me," Viktor reminded. "Off the record, of course. You've seen my pathology. You, of all people, know what I am."

"I will admit that you have a rare disease. We discussed this before." Three years ago, in fact. That's what Evan and his team had come to Boston to investigate. Nearly a month later, he was satisfied with his findings and he'd fallen in love during the course of that investigation. But fate had other plans for him. When he returned to Washington, an emergency had sent him and his team back into the trenches. They had barely gotten on the ground at the new site when a freak explosion at the private airfield ended the lives of every single person involved.

Except Evan Hunter.

"Have you checked your blood lately?" Viktor challenged. "I'll bet you have the same. Not only because of what occurred between the two of us, but because it was likely always there. You simply never had an awakening to make you aware of who you really were."

"What occurred between us," Evan shot back, "was

attempted murder." During the final hours of the investigation, both he and Viktor had snapped. They'd fought, both fully intending to kill the other, but Viktor had backed off, in all likelihood preventing Evan from committing murder. "We both wanted to kill each other."

"Agreed." Viktor moved to a sideboard on the far side of the room and poured himself a drink. He offered the same to Evan, but he declined. "You pushed me too far, Hunter. I had shown you the proof and still you would not believe. I was more angry than I can ever remember being."

"You showed me that you had a cult following," Evan returned, refusing to admit otherwise. "That there were people willing to believe your fantasies and commit to you for sexual gratification. Then, like now, one of your own kind sold you out."

That this bastard had touched Rowen in any fashion sent vengeance roaring through Evan's veins as fiercely as it had three years ago, made his brain throb with the need to explode.

"I cannot convince you, eh?" Viktor downed his liquor and set the glass aside. "Then let me tell you what I think is happening here. It is not, as you suggest, one of my *kind.*"

Viktor sauntered back to where Evan waited, his arrogance escalating. "I believe someone from your team leaked the truth about me and my followers. And now that someone is out to destroy us."

Evan was the one scoffing now. "Impossible. We told

no one. Our reports were highly classified, not to mention buried beneath mountains of red tape. If word got out, it didn't come from us."

"It must have," Viktor argued. "Not one of my followers would have dared speak of our existence."

"Why such unwavering faith? It happened before." This time Evan was the one sounding arrogant and smug.

Hatred burned in those dark eyes. "This time is different," Viktor said without hesitation. Three years ago, a band of his followers had gotten out of control, had gone on a feeding frenzy that brought unwanted attention to Viktor and his dark world.

"You talk about the truth," Evan confessed, knowing he should not do this but determined to end circular discussion. "I'll give you the truth. My team and I made a decision to leave the truth about you and your followers out of our final report. Meaning, there's nothing to find and no one to tell. All those involved with the investigation who knew this truth you speak of are dead."

"Except you," Viktor reminded.

Evan moved a step closer. "I have kept your secret as promised."

Viktor tilted his head questioningly, his smugness giving way to curiosity. "Why? You said yourself that you don't believe in our kind. What was your point?"

"To prevent those who would be foolish enough from turning a cult into a *breed*." There were plenty of people out there just looking for an excuse to believe in this kind of dark world. It wasn't real. Evan had no intention of making it real.

Evan surveyed the enormous room that was only one of many in Viktor's castle—the place, the atmosphere, all of it was just for show. Viktor wanted to believe he was a vampire, so he put on the whole dog and pony act. It made him feel better about the truth. He had a disease. One that required regular transfusions of fresh blood.

"That I can sense your thoughts, that I hardly age at all, none of this plays into your conclusions?"

"Lots of people have heightened senses," Evan argued. "That doesn't make them vampires. Aging is relative to the genes we inherit. You are who you are, a product of your ancestors."

Viktor was annoyed again but, to his credit, he remained visibly calm. "Mark my words, Hunter, the killer is one of yours."

"Perhaps," Evan allowed. "Just make sure you don't go after revenge. I don't think you want that kind of attention."

Viktor smiled. "Why, didn't you know? That's what you're here for." He shook his head slowly as amusement gained center stage in his expression. "You still don't understand. I spared your life three years ago because I had an epiphany. A vision, if you will."

"You spared my life," Evan said evenly, "because you knew if you didn't back off, I would kill you. Then we'd both be dead and this conversation wouldn't be taking place."

"Believe what you will, but there is a reason for everything, Hunter. I let you live and you survived that explosion because·fate knew that you were the only one who could stop this when the time came. That time is now. We are both here and it is happening."

"I guess we'll just have to agree to disagree." Evan fixed him with his a gaze that left no doubts as to what he meant when he added, "Just remember, Viktor, I'll be watching you and your people."

"What about your beautiful friend?"

A new jolt of outrage seared through Evan and he had to clench his hands tightly at his sides to hold back the cry of pain.

When it had passed he said from between clenched teeth, "Stay away from *Rowen* or I will end this for you. And this time, nothing will stop me." He turned to walk away. There was nothing more to say. He had to get back. Rowen was entirely too resourceful to leave unattended for long.

"You realize she is supposed to die, do you not?"

Evan turned slowly so as not to bring further suffering upon himself. He fought the crashing waves, but he was very near his breaking point. "Don't go near her again, Viktor."

"You won't be able to defend her much longer, my old friend," his nemesis said frankly. "You grow weaker. The medication takes its toll. Time is running out."

"I can still do what needs to be done," Evan threatened bluntly.

"There's only one cure besides the healing," Viktor tossed out to waylay him once more.

By healing, the bastard meant partaking of blood. He was truly convinced of his status as a vampire. He wanted Evan to believe he was one, as well.

Evan leveled his gaze back on the misguided man's. "And what cure is that?"

"Death," Viktor explained knowingly. "The only way to stop the overload of sensations you suffer without the healing is *death*. It's coming for you, Hunter, just as it is for your beloved."

ROWEN AWOKE TO A debilitating headache. She lay there for several seconds, hoping the worst would pass. When she reached down to throw back the covers, her hand froze and her mind grew still, focused inward.

This was not right.

Her eyes flew open and she blinked repeatedly to adjust. Where the hell was she?

The mattress, the texture of the covers, felt wrong.

When her vision had cleared, she sat up, then held her head in her hands until the room had stopped spinning. Taking slow, deep breaths, she focused all her senses on determining her current location.

A table lamp near the bed gave off a dim glow. A bedroom of some sort. The room's furnishings consisted of the bed and a side table and the one lamp.

Perhaps Viktor Azariel had somehow tricked her into

coming back to his castle…or maybe she'd never left at all. Had she dreamed the past few hours?

Fear slid through her veins with biting force, stealing her breath and her courage in one fell swoop.

No. She hadn't imagined anything. This, she glanced around the room, was real.

She threw back the covers and bounded out of the bed. A moment's recovery was required before she could walk, but as soon as the dizziness passed, she examined her prison. Checked the door. Moved from one window to the next to find each boarded shut behind the draperies preventing her from escaping, as well as seeing anything outside.

Inhaling deeply once, twice, she decided there was definitely an old smell, but not the same dank, cave-like smell of the ancient castle Viktor called home.

Okay. Windows boarded shut, door locked…

There had to be a way out of here.

Rowen suddenly stopped and stared down at herself. She wore her nightgown. The one she'd selected to put on after her bath last night. Or was it still night? But why couldn't she recall putting it on or going to bed? Had she dreamed the bath? The near drowning in her own tub? Was she still dreaming?

No, no. This didn't feel like a dream. She ran her fingers through her hair, tried to clear her mind.

The last thing she remembered was drinking the wine and falling asleep in the water. Almost drowning.

Well, she'd wanted some deep sleep; she'd definitely gotten that.

She froze.

Maybe she was dead.

"Slow down," she told herself. Deep breath. One more. No panicking. She wasn't dead. She just couldn't remember what had happened. Kind of like when she left Azariel's house. A little lost time. But she definitely wasn't dead. How crazy was it that a woman who solved murders for a living could be so damned afraid of dying herself? Not that anyone wanted to die, but this was an unreasonable fear…almost a warning that she had every reason to worry.

Forget that, she ordered. Focus on escape. She moved to the door. No sounds from the outside. No sounds inside, either.

She pressed her ear to the door that separated the room from God only knew what and listened. Nothing.

After searching the room from top to bottom, including under the bed, she found nothing. No purse. No clothes. No nothing. Just a few dust bunnies skittering across the wooden floor.

Disgusted and feeling weak again, she sat down on the edge of the bed and tried to remember the events of the previous night in chronological order.

Assuming it was the next morning at this point.

For all she knew, it could be the day after that.

Had another body been found?

Did Merv and the chief realize she was missing?

Oh, God, what about Princess?

She had to think.

She reviewed the whole day. She'd felt odd when she left Viktor's, couldn't account for those missing hours. Then had gone home. Walked Princess. Took a bath. The rest was blank until waking up just now.

Okay, rule out the less likely scenarios.

Since the windows were crudely boarded shut and she still wore her own nightgown, she hadn't been committed or admitted to any sort of hospital. And she definitely wasn't at home.

The place didn't smell like Viktor's castle, so he probably hadn't taken her hostage since she was on to his connection to two of the murder victims.

That left just one likelihood.

Hunter had kidnapped her. He'd been going on and on about how she wasn't safe. Maybe he'd slipped over some edge and taken her with him.

Panic knotted in her belly. She knew where that would lead. She stood and paced the room, wrestled with the building anxiety.

Walk it off. Let it go. Concentrate on the problem at hand. No panic attacks allowed.

She had to get out of this room.

What the hell was going on with Hunter? Had he lost his mind? Had he been in some sort of mental institution for the past three years?

Should she consider him a real threat?

Maybe so, she admitted, as she glanced around her prison.

Then again, maybe he hadn't nabbed her at all. Maybe it was the killer in the South End Murders case.

More of that tension worked its way through her insides. But they weren't even close to a suspect, discounting Viktor Azariel. But the killer might not know that.

If the killer wanted to get rid of her, why didn't he just erase the threat, murder her as he had the others?

She was back to motive.

No one dies for *naught.*

Dr. Forrester was right. And so was Azariel. There was a reason for these murders; she just hadn't found it yet. Hadn't latched on to the one tie that bound them all together in one neat little package. But that tie existed. She was certain of it.

The metal-on-metal click of the key turning in the lock wrenched her attention in that direction.

She looked around for a weapon, but there was nothing other than the pillows. Well, that would have to do. She grabbed the closest one and used it like a shield. Steeled herself for fighting her opponent.

The door opened and Hunter stepped into the room.

"You son of a bitch!" She slammed him with the pillow. He flinched as if it actually hurt.

"What the hell do you think you're doing?" She lit into him again, banging him on every side with the fluffy weapon. She wanted to hurt him. This wasn't going to get the job done and, yet, she couldn't control the frenzy that had overtaken her.

He snatched the pillow from her hand and threw it back onto the bed. Rowen fought to catch her breath…to calm herself and think rationally.

"When you can talk reasonably, I'll be back."

"Wait!" she cried when he was about to walk out and close the door again. She couldn't let that happen.

He hesitated, his eyes still hidden with those confounding dark glasses.

"What're you doing, Hunter?" She spoke calmly despite the wrath and confusion whirling inside her. "What happened to you?" He was a former FBI agent. Was at the top of his career three years ago. How had he fallen so far?

"I warned you that you were in danger," he offered flatly. Where was the emotion? Where was the man she used to know…the man she had loved?

"And this is supposed to help?" she demanded. "I have five murders to solve, in case you didn't notice. People are dying. I need to be back out there on the streets doing what I do."

"You're not safe out there. This is the only way to protect you."

"Who's going to protect me from you?" She dared to move closer, wasn't actually physically afraid of him. Not really. "You're the only one causing me trouble, Hunter."

"You don't have all the information you need to make an informed decision."

When he was about to depart and close the door behind him, she threw herself in his path. "Don't you dare lock me up in here again!"

"You'll have to trust me, *Rowen*. I know that can't be easy for you considering our past, but it's your only option."

"Can't be easy for me!" Okay, that pushed her over the line of reason. "You make me fall in love with you and then you walk away? You already left me with only one option, Hunter. The option of forgetting you existed." She shook her head, still unable to believe his nerve. "Then you suddenly show up here again and expect me to just fall for whatever line you throw my way?"

"We'll talk again later," he repeated, clearly vexed by her determination not to believe him.

"No!" She refused to move. "We'll talk now."

She felt him analyzing her from beneath those dark shades. He wasn't sure just how far she would push. Well, he'd better understand this now—she would not be treated like a prisoner.

"Are you hungry?"

Hungry? He was out of his mind. That was the only logical explanation. When she was about to launch into him with another tirade, she remembered Princess. "How can you expect me to eat when my dog is at home alone with no food?"

Incredibly, that appeared to give him pause.

"I can't believe you didn't think of that. I have to go home or my dog will starve."

Rowen barely stepped back in time for the door to close in her face.

So much for the sympathy ploy.

Chapter Eight

Rowen had spent at least an hour walking the floor.

She'd tried to pick the lock on the door with the short metal spoke she'd ripped from the lampshade where it attached to the top of the lamp base. Then she'd exhausted herself in an attempt to pry the boards from the windows.

Nothing had worked. The metal spoke wasn't rigid enough and she wasn't strong enough.

Having admitted defeat on that level, she considered her only other option—be prepared to physically fight her way out of here when Hunter returned.

If he returned.

It was the only way.

With that decision made, she waited. Distracted herself with details of the investigation. Merv and the chief would surely recognize that she was missing in action by now.

She didn't need those two distracted by her disappearance. Someone had to be focused on this deranged killer before he struck again.

Her hands moved up to chafe her chilly arms as she thought about the brutal crime scenes from the past week. Guilt plagued her when she considered that her discomfort was nothing compared to what those victims had endured at the hands of some psychotic monster. What had made him choose those particular victims?

Only two that she was aware of were connected to Viktor Azariel. Could the others have been involved with him on some level she hadn't discovered yet? Could she trust anything he told her? Common sense told her he would leave out anything incriminating.

One thing was certain—she couldn't do anything from here. She surveyed the cramped room once more.

Frustration fired through her. Surely Hunter would come back. He wouldn't leave her here like this.

Then again, maybe he would.

The grind of the key in the lock had her wheeling toward the door.

He was back.

Relief flooded her, but trepidation followed right on its heels. He was far bigger than her. Did she even stand a chance escaping? At least he'd come back. She should be thankful for that at least, she supposed, but the only emotion she could muster was fury. It burned away any misgivings she'd experienced.

Feet spread shoulder width apart, she adopted a defensive stance as he pushed the door inward.

The instant her eyes verified that it was, indeed, Hunter, some rogue cell misfired and her self-defense mode shifted into offense. She had to get out of here, one way or another.

With that in mind, she slugged him. Put every ounce of weight she had into the punch.

He staggered.

Pain splintered up her arm. Her fingers throbbed.

But, damn, it felt good.

Victory withered and died in the next instant.

He held on to the door as if that was all that kept him vertical. The bag he'd been carrying dropped to the floor. His breathing heaved in and out erratically, but the one thing that unnerved her the most was his attempt to restrain the soft grunts of pain.

She'd hurt him.

Really hurt him.

Damn.

Part of her wanted to make a run for it while he was down for the count, but the part of her that still cared for him couldn't do it. She reached out to him. He flinched when her hand landed on his arm. She drew back, anger almost overtaking her softer emotions again. What was with that? Did he despise her touch that much? Or was he concerned she would attempt another assault on him?

Where was that big tough guy she'd come to know?

He straightened. Visibly pulled himself back together. "Your dog is fine," he said, his voice weary, breathless. "I took care of her needs." He kicked the bag on the floor toward her. "I brought this for you."

He'd taken care of Princess and what had she done? She'd slugged him. Her first instinct was to apologize. God, he seemed so vulnerable. This was Hunter…how was that possible? But three years of bitterness overrode that initial instinct and she grabbed the bag and backed away from him without so much as a thank-you.

"I need a bathroom." Good thinking, she told herself. Just get out of this room. Forget all the other stuff clamoring for her attention.

Truth was, she could use a bathroom.

He stepped back from the door. "This way." He gestured to his left.

Rowen eased out into a dimly lit corridor. She looked around, determined that the bedroom was above the first level, maybe even the second, of wherever the hell they were.

"Next door on your right," he told her.

She nodded and moved in that direction. If he let her go in alone, there could be items in there that she could use as weapons. Hurting him again wasn't her goal, but if that's what it took…

Anticipation influenced the rhythm of her heart as she closed and locked the door behind her. She had to get out of here.

Blinds filtered the natural light from the small window near the toilet. She dropped the bag and slipped over to it, parted the blinds and peered out.

She was on a third floor, she decided after judging the distance down to the ground. No trees or roof structures for jumping out onto, assuming she could wiggle through the cramped opening.

It was daylight, but still early. The grass and trees looked damp with morning dew. Assuming she hadn't slept through a full twenty-four hour period, she might not be missed at all yet.

The area around her prison was wooded for as far as she could see. There were no distinctive features that lent even a remote clue as to where the hell she might be. She didn't recognize a damned thing.

But what little she'd learned helped. She had an idea of her distance from the city—well outside Boston proper. Without a vehicle, she was likely trapped, even if she did manage to get away from the house.

After searching the bathroom and finding nothing, she took care of nature's call and then washed her face. The bag still sat on the floor where she'd left it. She reached down and retrieved it, only then recognizing it as an overnight bag from her own closet.

Inside she found two pair of jeans, three blouses, sneakers, socks and toiletries. She pulled out a clean pair of panties and she was instantly transported back to three years ago. He'd been the handsomest man she'd ever met. Attentive, intriguing. Just damned interesting. She'd been infatuated with him immediately.

But he'd walked away. Left her to deal with how deeply she'd fallen for him.

She didn't want him touching her or her things.

Anger clicked her bitterness switch and she suddenly

wanted to slug him again, just to see if she could hurt him the way he'd hurt her. It wasn't bad enough he'd turned her world upside down three years ago; he had to show up now and hold her hostage. Obviously he'd intended to keep her here awhile, judging by the items he'd packed.

Allowing her anger to build and smolder, she took her time, washed up, pulled on fresh clothes, then brushed her hair. She didn't usually wear makeup, so it didn't matter that he hadn't brought any.

She bundled up the gown and undies she'd shed and stuffed them into the bag. She left bag and all on the chair next to the porcelain sink and opened the door, determined to find a way to escape her jailer.

"Did you find everything you needed?" he asked as she stepped into the hall where he waited. She couldn't be sure if the question was sincere or if he wanted her to know he realized what she'd been doing rummaging around in there.

"Everything but my Glock," she told him frankly. "If I had it, I could end this right now."

He showed no outward reaction to her remark. She wondered if he still carried a weapon. What was she thinking? Of course he did. This was Hunter. Ace special agent. That coat could conceal several weapons.

"There's food downstairs if you'd like to eat."

She folded her arms over her chest. "Sure. I want to keep up my strength. I'm going to need it when I take you down, Hunter. Because you are going down for this."

Again, he chose not to respond. But since he was on

to her machinations, he now insisted she go first when they descended the stairs.

The first staircase was narrow and led straight down. The door at the bottom opened into a second hallway at the end, of which a more traditional staircase led down to a first-floor entry hall.

Judging by the wood trim, floors and architecture, the house was at least a century old. But that didn't tell her anything. There were tons of old houses just like this in the Boston area. The woods that surrounded the property gave far more information. She wondered if they were in the Berkshires near Azariel's estate, but she couldn't be sure.

Like the bedroom where she'd been held prisoner, the rest of the house was spartanly furnished. The absolute bare essentials. The smell of the place suggested that it stayed closed up a good portion of the time.

In contrast to her kitchen back home, this one hadn't been revamped since it had been built, but it looked clean enough. A rental, she decided. Summer rental, considering the lingering odor of disuse.

A sandwich and soup waited for her. The packaging indicated it had been purchased at a deli near her home. That the soup was still warm surprised her. Maybe they weren't so far from the city. She'd tried to get a look out the windows she had passed en route to the kitchen, but all were shrouded in heavy draperies.

Speaking of shrouded, the fact that Hunter still wore that long black coat and the dark glasses tugged at her curiosity.

As much as she wanted to be rid of him, especially at the moment, she also wanted desperately to know what had happened to him.

For now, she ate. Strength was necessary for what lay ahead of her. She didn't need to be distracted by hunger pains or the weakness that went hand in hand with going without proper nourishment.

As she finished off the soup, she suddenly pondered the idea that he could have put more drugs in there. Her hand paused halfway to her mouth. She should have thought of that sooner. He'd no doubt drugged her in order to get her here.

Her gaze drifted to Hunter, who was sitting directly across the table watching her. Why the hell hadn't she thought of that already? Where were her usually dependable instincts?

"There's nothing in your food," he said, reading her mind as effectively as if she'd asked the question aloud.

Annoyed at his ability to read her so thoroughly, and still ravenous, she devoured the rest of the sandwich. She wished she could see his eyes. She could feel him watching her and she didn't like that he hid his thoughts from her so well when she couldn't do the same.

When she'd finished eating, she cleaned up, all under his watchful gaze, despite her inability to see his eyes. He followed her movements and that was indication enough that his complete attention was on her.

"Now can we talk?" she asked. He'd remained silent,

save for that one statement, throughout the course of her meal.

She needed answers. She needed to know what had possessed a man who had once been a highly respected agent in the Bureau to kidnap an officer of the law, ultimately preventing her from working on an ongoing case. A high-profile one at that—with five murder victims.

"I won't change my mind," he warned, his mouth firm with resolve.

Dammit, she'd give most anything to see his eyes. To read what he was thinking.

Surely the man she'd loved so desperately hadn't turned into some sort of madman.

"I want to see your eyes, Hunter."

Somehow the words had come out of her with more neediness than she wanted him to hear…but it was too late to worry about it now.

For half a dozen frantic beats of her heart, she wasn't sure he intended to respond, but then he stood. "Come with me."

She wanted to look for a knife, anything with which to defend herself, but there was no time…and, quite honestly, it felt wrong. Completely wrong.

There was no way Hunter wanted to hurt her. Whatever he was doing, he felt compelled to do in order to protect her. Barring, of course, the idea that he had suffered some sort of mental breakdown.

He showed her the way to what appeared to be a parlor or den. Dark, shadowy…very much like the man.

The windows were scarcely distinguishable from the walls, both were clad in a deep mahogany hue, almost a black.

He closed the double doors that led into the entry hall and Rowen couldn't help a shudder. The smell of age and mustiness dredged up images of past lives and ghosts who purportedly haunted houses like this.

Now she was falling victim to the Halloween craze. Just what she needed.

She waited in the middle of the room, standing, though the usual conversational grouping of a sofa and two chairs flanked a fireplace. She didn't want to sit, needed to be ready in the event an opportunity presented itself.

When Hunter turned to face her, she looked to him expectantly. She didn't understand his hesitation. Was he scarred? Was that the reason for the heavy clothing? Had his vision been affected somehow?

The thought of the kind of scars fire could leave behind and the subsequent tenderness made her wince inwardly at the idea that she'd hurt him…purposely hurt him. Had he suffered some devastating accident? Fire could have damaged his vision, as well.

She swallowed, her throat tight with indecision. She didn't know whether to feel sorry for him or to be angry as hell at his impudence.

Slowly, his hands moved up to his face and he removed the concealing eyewear. Evan blinked a couple of times but with the room this dimly lit, it wasn't intolerable.

Rowen stared at him, waiting to see what he would reveal.

He settled his gaze on her now, let her see what she would. What he saw was very nearly his undoing. The glimmer of uncertainty in her eyes, the distant hope for something he refused to broach. There was a time when he had loved looking at her. So beautiful, even now, in well-worn jeans and a simple tee. She would have been even more beautiful naked…he remembered well how she looked. Dreamed of her often.

But such dreams were a mistake. Only made his existence more unendurable.

She moved closer. His heart reacted, sending the resulting tremors of angst through his soul.

"Your eyes look…the same," she said after a thorough scrutiny. "Why do you wear those glasses?"

He shoved the eyewear into his coat pocket and mulled over how best to approach this answer.

"You can see all right, can't you?"

"I see perfectly." He did. He saw the way she looked at him. Rowen would have him believe that she hated him now and some part of her did. She was bitter and resentful of the time they had shared and how much it had cost her. But she still cared for him. He ached to foster that…to hold her as he had before. But that would only condemn them both to the hell he'd awoken to three years ago. That was why he hadn't returned to her…why he never could. And he had paid dearly for that decision. But his own pain in no way assuaged his guilt for having hurt her.

He should never have come back…but she'd needed him. Rowen simply didn't understand it yet.

She moved nearer still. He braced for what she would say or whatever sudden attempt she might make to escape him.

"Your face looks just like before," she said softly, her eyes still studying him.

Then she reached up…he drew back.

Her hand fell away and she shook her head, fury kindling in her eyes. "Why do you do that?"

The pain behind the anger in her voice twisted his insides into knots of agony. She misunderstood his dread of her touch.

"Contact is uncomfortable for me," he admitted, his tone guttural with his own pain, part physical, part mental. How could he do this to himself? Bringing her here like this…being with her was like being poleaxed over and over again. Like her, he still had feelings, feelings he had kept carefully compartmentalized. Until now. Until this moment, when he wanted so desperately to touch her.

"So if I touch you in any way it hurts?"

He nodded, not trusting his voice.

She clasped her hands behind her back as if she feared her inability to restrain them, then moistened her lips. "Then I'll be careful not to do that." She inhaled sharply. "I'm sorry. When I slugged you it must have been—"

"It doesn't hurt now," he hastened to assure her. He didn't want her feeling guilty for any of this. It wasn't her fault.

She closed her eyes and visibly fought her emotions. "Hunter." She opened those beautiful honey-brown eyes once more and looked deeply into his. "Tell me what happened to you."

"There was an explosion," he explained. "The rest of my team was killed. I survived, but there were side effects from the intense trauma."

"You had some sort of brain injury?" she prodded, logic leading her.

"Yes. Senses heightened to the point of pain. My hearing in particular. Something as simple as a breaking glass can be excruciating."

She nodded her understanding, remembering the incident in her kitchen. "There's nothing they can do?"

"A partial lobotomy," he said derisively, "but the risk of being turned into a living vegetable was an even worse scenario, so I refused."

"It must be awful for you." She considered what he'd told her for a few moments, then asked, "Is this why you didn't come back?"

His heart started to race. He tried to slow it, but it was no use. The sound of his own blood roaring through his veins was deafening, but even that could not detract from how badly he wanted to tell her…to see the forgiveness in her eyes. But that would be wrong. He knew Rowen too well. She would stick by him in spite of his curse. Then her life would be doomed to this hell as surely as his own was.

He cleared all emotion from his eyes and let her believe the lie he uttered to be truth. "No. I made that decision before the accident happened. There was no room in my life for commitment."

She drew back with the impact of his words. Hurt filled her eyes before she blinked it away. She'd wanted to believe that she finally had a justifiable reason for the way he'd walked away and he'd snatched it from her—for her own good. Just as his holding her here was for her own safety.

"Whatever you think you're doing, Hunter," she said, her voice trembling with anger and remnants of the other emotions she didn't want to feel, "you have to release me now. Let me go without further argument and I won't press charges. Pursue this crazy scheme and you'll be doing time in Devens."

"If I let you go," he said cautiously, aware that he'd lost any gained ground, "you'll end up dead. I won't let that happen."

Her face tightened with fury. "I'm a homicide detective. I deal with danger all the time. It's what I do. You're obstructing justice here, Hunter. I have a case I should be working on." Her voice rose with each statement, making her all the angrier. She looked away, grappled to regain some semblance of composure.

A wave of dizziness assaulted him and he had to close his eyes to ward it off. The medication was wearing off. Soon he would be forced to take another dose. He couldn't waste his energy arguing about this.

She waited for him to look at her once more. The impatience radiating from her put him on edge. "Get out of my way, Hunter."

He braced for the coming fight. "I can't let you go."

A rasp of disgust issued from her throat. "You walk away from me and expect me to believe that whether I live or die matters to you? Get real, Hunter. I don't know what kind of game you're playing, but I'm not going to participate. Now, step aside."

"No."

And then she did the last thing he would have expected in a million years—she moved in on him and hung her arms around his neck. She snuggled her body close to his and let him feel every womanly curve and contour. His mind reeled with the abrupt about-face.

"Well," she said with a sigh, "if I'm stuck here, we might as well make the best of it." Her fingers crept down to his shirtfront and began, one by one, releasing the buttons of his shirt.

A tremor of want went through him, but he knew what she was doing. But knowing that and getting it through to his body proved beyond his ability. The crash of excitement into his brain almost took his breath. The pleasure-pain was nearly unbearable. He wanted to feel her hands on his skin…wanted to touch her all over, but the results would be more than he could endure. He knew that outcome would likely destroy him and still he yearned for exactly that.

He had to be strong.

He manacled her arms to push her away. She tiptoed

and, aiming for his mouth, she kissed his jaw when he turned his head. The feel of her soft lips on his skin sent a shockwave of emotion roiling through him. He couldn't think, could only feel the intensifying sensations flooding his system, dragging him downward into a spiral of pure sensory mania.

Somehow, she wrestled one arm from his loosening grip and before he could react snagged his weapon from his shoulder holster.

"Move away from the door," she ordered as she backed away from him, the weapon aimed center chest.

His head was still spinning with emotions and sensations he hadn't allowed himself to feel in years. He stood his ground.

"I can't do that." His voice sounded rusty and depleted.

"Step aside or I will shoot," she warned. She'd latched on to the weapon with both hands now and released the safety, her feet spread apart for balance. He had no doubt she meant business.

"Then shoot." There was no fighting it. He'd pushed too far. He needed another round of the medication. Couldn't hold his own with her any longer. If she shot him, it would be over. But then who would keep her safe?

She took a wary step in his direction, her eyes distrustful, her aim steady. "Take off your coat." She gestured for him to do it now. "I want to make sure this weapon is the only one you're carrying."

Other than the knife in his boot, that was it. But she

didn't know that and, like any good cop, would only believe what her eyes told her.

He shouldered out of the coat, allowed it to drop to the floor. Knowing what she wanted without having to be asked, he stepped away from the door and turned all the way around. He moved very slowly to ensure his balance and to stave off another surge of pain.

"Don't move." She placed a hand on his shoulder while his back was to her. Setting off more of those pleasure-pain sensations, she patted him down. Didn't forego a single step in the process. The feel of her hands as she felt up his loins made him shudder…made him want to come inside her then and there. Memories of doing just that flooded his mind, bringing him to a whole new level of agony.

He couldn't let this happen.

She was as lost to him as his life was, but he would die protecting her.

"Now. Step away from the door."

He turned around slowly to face her. She'd moved out of his reach, so there was no hope of getting a grip on her again. It wasn't so much that he believed she wouldn't shoot him as it was his desperation to save her that had him frantically racking his brain for his next move. He had to do something before she acted on her threat.

"Move, Hunter," she reiterated, "or I'll shoot."

"Shoot," he baited. "I'm not letting you go."

Frustration joined the fury making her heart pound,

making her want to do just as he suggested. He watched the dance of emotions across her face and it hurt him to see the painful disillusionment.

"Don't make me do this, Hunter." This time, her tone was pleading.

He saw the glint of hurt in her eyes. She wasn't going to back off. Not this time. But it was killing her to force the issue.

"I can't do that," he admitted. There was no way he could hide the depth of his own emotions from her. She got a good look. Her eyes rounded as she processed what she saw in his.

The high-pitched chimes of a cellular phone interrupted the silence that followed.

Evan went on guard, knew exactly whose phone it was and where it had come from. The sound pierced him with more shards of torment.

"That's my phone," she said, startled.

He didn't bother responding.

"Where is it?" She surveyed the room, noting the empty, open shelves that lined the wall and the tattered sofa and chairs.

Evan set his jaw, refused to say a word.

"Screw you," she hissed as she followed the sound, keeping one eye, as well as a bead, on him.

By ring three she'd located her purse tucked beneath the sofa and fished out the cell phone.

She wrenched it open. "O'Connor."

He didn't have to hear the other side of the conversation—though he certainly could have had the medication not dulled his sense of hearing so well—to understand that the call represented a new devastating layer to this nightmare. All he had to do was watch the evolving expressions setting her face in stone.

"I'll be right there." She closed the phone and turned to Evan. "My partner's been trying to reach me."

The remote quality of her tone set his instincts on point. He waited for her to say the rest.

"There's been another murder." She blinked as shock and disbelief settled more fully in her expression. "Finch…the new detective assigned to my team. He's dead."

Evan moved toward her then. She was shaken to the core. And why not? One of her own—a cop—was dead at the hands of a ruthless killer.

"He was found at home this morning." She shook her head. "Just like the others. It's crazy."

With Evan's final approach, she scrambled back to attention, took aim at him. "Back off," she snarled.

He laid his hand on her arm, pushed the barrel of the weapon away from his chest and said, "I'll take you there, *Rowen.* But you have to let me stay close."

As much as he wanted to keep her here…as desperately as he wanted to keep her safe…there was no backing away from the case now.

Whether Rowen realized it yet, this new murder was another message.

This time, it was for her.

Chapter Nine

Jeff Finch had lived at Braddock Park, one of the leafy residential squares that peppered the South End in distinctive Boston flair. Certainly not the typical place one looked for a gruesome murder or even a cop, unless he inherited well or married better. Long narrow gardens with a splashing fountain or two enclosed by wrought-iron railings welcomed residents to the two- and three-story brick row houses.

It was the perfect New England setting, with autumn-colored leaves dancing in the morning breeze beneath the watchful eyes of low-browed windows. Balustrades and decorative iron railings around windows and balconies overlooked the street, offering a sense of heritage and beauty.

But today, that lovely scene was marred by strips of yellow police tape and pulsing blue lights from the Boston PD cruisers sitting askew along the block.

Shocked citizens, all looking fit and stylish, watched from the sidewalk on the opposite side of the

street. The presence of the medical examiner's van
was ominous.

Death had dared to visit their gentrified neighborhood. And the vultures swarmed. News vans and reporters encroached as far as the uniforms would allow into
off-limits territory.

Inside, where curious eyes could not see, Finch's
body was posed in bed. Rowen understood now that the
killer had chosen the position as meticulously as he had
the method of delivering death. Naked save for the pris-
tine white sheet covering the lower part of his anatomy,
Finch's face bore the look of startled defeat he'd no
doubt felt when he realized the end was inevitable.

As in Ellen Green's case, the blood drained from
him had been left at the scene rather than taken away.
It had made a path down the left side of his chest and
coagulated in a wide crimson pool around his buttocks.

There were no signs of a struggle. Nothing appeared
to be missing, but his only next of kin—his widowed
mother, in ill health and living in Arizona—would be
walked through the apartment later to confirm that.

Rowen crouched next to the bed and studied Finch
from a different perspective. He was a cop, for God's
sake. Why hadn't he struggled?

Merv was busy overseeing the interviews of neighbors. Doherty was puking in the en suite bathroom. Apparently he and Finch had become good pals over the
past few days. Or maybe they'd known each other before.

What the hell did this mean? Rowen wondered.

Finch couldn't have been a donor...

Dr. Cost and his assistant moved to the side of the bed nearest the victim. "Any reason I can't begin?" Cost asked Rowen without bothering to shift his attention from the corpse he'd already started to evaluate visually.

She shook her head and stood. Her gaze latched on to Cost's. "You know what to look for."

He nodded, his expression somber.

If Finch was a donor, she needed to know ASAP.

Hunter came up behind her. She didn't have to turn around. She could feel his presence. Merv hadn't liked that she'd allowed him on the scene. Explaining her motivation would have taken too long. Even she wasn't sure she understood why she'd let Hunter get to her like this. He'd taken her hostage, had held her against her will for at least twelve hours. And what had she done? Fallen for his ploy, as if he hadn't already jerked the rug out from under her feet once.

Probably another mistake.

But this case was too important to allow anything or anyone to get in the way. And she knew Hunter. He would not have relented in his quest to protect her.

"Viktor has been here," Hunter murmured for her ears only.

Despite her desire to watch Cost's examination, she turned to Hunter. "How can you be certain?"

She couldn't see his eyes for those confounded glasses, but she heard the conviction in his voice when he spoke. "I can smell him."

Rowen barely hung on to her composure, choosing not to question the response. As hard as she tried to hold it back, a shudder went through her at the idea that he could be right. Probably was. "Do your instincts tell you that the two were connected?"

"No. Viktor was following the killer."

Rowen swore softly. "Why didn't he tell us that he knew the killer's identity?" If Azariel knew this bastard, he needed to come clean so they could nail the guy.

"I'm not sure," Hunter admitted.

She worried her bottom lip with her teeth. She hated to ask the question, but her curiosity got the better of her. Not once in her life had she allowed herself to believe such things, but here she was about to show she could. "What about the killer? Do you sense anything about him?"

Hunter turned away from her a moment. She wished she could see his eyes, analyze his thinking. She hated being so removed from his feelings. But then, hadn't she always been? She simply hadn't known how far off the mark she really had been three years ago. That same old bitterness attempted to rear its ugly head, but she tamped it down. Now was not the time. Finch was dead. Five other people were dead, as well. They deserved her full attention.

When Hunter rested his shielded gaze back on hers, he said, "I sense something else, but it's too vague to be sure." He surveyed the room. "The sensation is familiar. Whoever did this is someone I've met before. And it has something to do with you and me. That much I'm certain of."

What could any of this have to do with her or him? Rowen turned back to where Cost and his assistant were prepping the body for transport.

She hadn't even met Finch until a couple days ago. She hadn't known any of the other victims. Hunter's conclusion didn't make sense. He'd been out of the Bureau for three years. What reason could anyone have for luring him back to Boston? The only connection she and Hunter had was their affair. And, clearly, it had been just an affair.

"He's baiting us," Hunter whispered, reading her mind again. "That's why the first murder was conducted on a night and in a jurisdiction where you would be sure to get the call. As have all the others."

That was crazy.

"You think Viktor is trying to lure me into some kind of trap?"

That didn't make sense, either. What did she have to do with him or his bizarre cult of vampire worshippers? Nothing. She'd been remotely aware some people took the whole vampire, witch and werewolf business to the extreme, but she hadn't known anyone in particular.

"Not Viktor. He's as much a pawn or target in this as you."

A thought poked through the haze of confusion. "What about you?" She set her hands on her jean-clad hips. She wasn't dressed appropriately for work, but there had been no time to change. "What do you have to do with this?"

The tension thickened between them for half a minute.

"I came here for you," he said frankly. "I sensed you were in danger and I came to protect you. Whoever is doing this knew I would."

"So it's you who's been following me?" Ire twisted through her. She needed coffee. She didn't need him cluttering her reasoning.

"Yes."

"Detective?"

Rowen issued him one last glare, then turned to join Dr. Cost near the victim.

Finch's body was almost fully uncovered now. She resisted the urge to look away. The guy had prided himself on the way he dressed. He wouldn't like this. Murder was so damned humiliating.

"I think you'd better take a look at his," Cost suggested.

Dread collected in her gut. Surely he hadn't found the tattoo. As a cop, Finch had to have been way too logical to get caught up in something as illogical as vampirism. She watched as Cost moved the sheet farther down Finch's lower extremities.

On the white linen, between his spread legs, starting at his ankles, words were scrawled in red blood.

The woman is next.

Her knees gave way, but she caught herself before losing her balance completely.

"Was Detective Finch married or involved with anyone?" Cost asked.

Rowen shook her head. It wouldn't have mattered anyway; she knew what the message meant.

She was next.

As Rowen and Hunter exited the building, reporters shouted questions, except she was in no mood to answer. Bulbs flashed from cameras. She felt Hunter flinch next to her and she suddenly wished she could protect him from this. The morning sun, which had finally poked a hole in the gloomy cloud cover, had to be giving him trouble already.

The crowd of onlookers had been joined by those wearing Goth attire and carrying signs welcoming the vampires to Boston. Idiots. Didn't they realize a man was dead inside? Or did they just not care?

Just when the urge to scream almost had become too great to subdue, Hunter ushered her into his vehicle.

He backed away from the curb. Reporters followed, pushing and shoving, to get the last shot of the lead detective leaving the scene empty-handed and with an unidentified male. They would make something of that.

She didn't care. Her only concern right now was the fact that she had nothing.

Not the first damned lead.

Six people were dead.

Including one of Boston's finest.

Her jaw clenched and she fought to stem the overriding emotions.

Another ten, maybe fifteen, minutes passed before she shook off the disturbing thoughts. She realized then that Hunter was headed in the wrong direction.

"There's a postmortem with the chief and Merv at One Schroeder Plaza. I have to be there."

The mayor, every damned body, would want something *now.* She could only hope Cost would find something in the autopsy that would provide some insight. Otherwise, she would be looking for a new job. But there was no reason to believe the M.E. would find anything at all. He hadn't found a single thing so far other than the tattoo; she doubted he would now. The one and only clue any of these murders had yielded was that damned tattoo and it had only taken them as far as Azariel. Merv hadn't found a tattoo artist in any parlor in the city who would own up to having done the ones the victims sported or even similar ones. No one wanted to get involved in this dirty business.

"I understand your need to meet with your chief," Evan said, "but first we need to pay Viktor a visit." He didn't bother explaining that he knew for certain now that Viktor knew a great deal more than he was sharing. Evan intended to have the truth, one way or another. He didn't like bringing Rowen along, but he couldn't, especially now, risk letting her out of his sight for a second. He also knew her. She would reach the same conclusions. He didn't want her attempting to give him the slip and doing this very thing.

She didn't argue. That alone spoke volumes about her state of mind. One of her own was dead. And she understood what the message the killer had left behind meant. *She was next on the kill list.*

Evan gritted his teeth. He would not let that happen.

Rain had started to fall, streaking the windshield of his rented car. Darkness amassed in the sky, providing relief from the sun for him, but giving Boston the dismal look of a city grieving for its loss. A city under siege by unknown sinister forces.

The city looked murky, depressed…and eerily crying out for justice.

The killing had to stop. Evan had to see to that.

HARDLY AWARE of the time passing, Rowen was startled back to attention as they turned into the long drive of the Azariel estate. The lush landscaping didn't look so attractive tonight. The meticulously groomed shrubs formed dark, somber statues in the night. She felt as if she'd stumbled into a scene from *Dawn of the Dead.* Not a good feeling.

The few seconds it took to hustle up the massive stone steps and reach the towering entry doors of Azariel's castle proved sufficient for the wind to cut straight to the bone. She shivered. Hunter tried to shield her, even offered his coat, but she refused. She understood that the coat protected him somehow. She would not be the cause of more pain for him. As much as she'd thought she'd wanted to do just that, she had been wrong. No matter how much she wanted to hate him, merely looking at him like this weakened her resolve.

He didn't bother with lifting the enormous door knocker, he just entered the castle as if he lived there.

Rowen swallowed back her trepidation and followed him. She wondered vaguely where the butler was. He usually showed up on the steps in anticipation of her arrival. Surely the guard at the gate had alerted the household to the unexpected arrival of company.

Hunter looked in the parlor first. It was deserted.

"Maybe we should call out to him," Rowen suggested. They were trespassing. Anything they discovered would be inadmissible in a court of law considering they had no warrant of search and seizure. Not to mention the place gave her the creeps. The last time she'd been here, she'd lost several hours of her life.

Hunter shot a look in her direction and it wasn't necessary to see his eyes to know she should just let him do what he wanted. The grim line of his lips and the hard set of his jaw said plenty.

She trudged up the stairs behind him and ascertained that their destination was Viktor's suite. She shuddered. At the cold, she told herself. The biting October wind didn't go well with this damned cave of a dwelling. Whispered voices echoed in the upstairs hall, but she had to have imagined them since no one was around. She hoped she imagined the sounds.

Okay. Pull it together. She wasn't usually a fraidy cat on the job. She reserved that for home.

The feeling that someone had come up behind her had her pivoting to look. Nothing.

When she turned back to Hunter he waited outside the double doors that led to Viktor's suite.

"Are you coming?"

Rowen hurried to catch up to him. She didn't have her gun. What the hell was she doing here unarmed and unprepared for a confrontation?

She should have made Hunter take her to One Schroeder Plaza, should have demanded they stop by her house for her weapon. Her fingers tightened on the strap of her purse where it draped over her shoulder. She did have her cell phone. She should call for backup.

Before she could express that opinion, Hunter pushed open the doors and strode into the sitting room that served as a reception area for Viktor's bedroom.

Viktor stood near the fireplace, as if he'd anticipated their arrival and had lit a fire for their comfort.

He looked directly at Rowen. "Come, Detective—warm yourself."

Hunter held up a hand for her to stay put. Rowen looked from him to Viktor.

"Come now, Hunter," Viktor said, "you mustn't deny the good detective a place by the fire. She's freezing. Can't you see?"

As if on cue, Rowen shivered.

A twitch of Hunter's fingers gave her permission to join Viktor at the fire.

Strangely, she obeyed. The heat reached out to her like a beacon, drew her across the room. She held out her hands to warm them. Maybe later she would contemplate why she'd allowed Hunter to rule her in any capacity, but right now she was just too weary and cold to care. That Viktor stood beside her was of no consequence.

"You were there," Hunter accused.

"I was."

Rowen watched as the two men moved to the center of the room and appeared to square off.

For the third time that morning, she wished she had her Glock.

She turned from the inviting flames and monitored the evolving scene, her heart thundering. Her mind screamed at her to intervene, but some deeply entrenched survival instinct kept her nailed to the spot.

"Did you kill him?" Hunter demanded softly.

The ferocity of his words made Rowen shiver again.

Viktor laughed just lethally. "Now, why would I do that? Had Finch been a donor, I would have been cutting off my own right arm. Since he was not, what would have been the point?"

"Explain your presence." Another quietly issued command.

Viktor moved in closer to Hunter. Rowen tensed. Too close. Viktor did not appear to be armed, but he was way too close for comfort.

"You know why I was there, brother."

The reference Viktor used startled Rowen. What the hell did he mean by *brother*? Her gaze flew back to Hunter. Apparently it didn't sit well with him, either.

Hunter said something else to Viktor, something

crude that perfectly sized up what he thought of the man's referring to him so intimately.

"I was there," Viktor intoned—he hadn't backed off; neither had Hunter—"to verify the identity of the killer you seek."

"Why would I trust your conclusions?" Hunter asked archly. "You pretend to be so self-righteous when the truth is you prey on those who are weaker, just as this killer does."

The smile that slid across Viktor's mouth then made Rowen's respiration stutter. There was no question the man was good-looking in a dark, mysterious way, but this smile was pure evil. Fear snaked around her heart.

"Look deep inside yourself, Hunter, and you will find your killer," Viktor returned with just as much disgust and hatred as Hunter had offered.

Was he trying to say that Hunter had committed these murders? Each time Hunter had shown up after the fact, after a murder. Did he have an alibi for the murders?

Wait. This was Hunter. She shook herself. He wouldn't kill anyone. She knew him better than that.

But did she? Really? He'd told her about the explosion. Serious brain trauma had resulted. Brain injuries changed people. He wasn't the same man she had known.

Then again, her gaze shifting to Viktor, she didn't know him at all. He'd drugged her or hypnotized her that time. She certainly couldn't trust him.

Flashes of memory slammed into her brain next.

Viktor moving over her…his breath whispering against her skin.

No. She closed her eyes and suppressed the images. She couldn't be sure that had really happened. It hadn't, she told herself. A dream. No, a nightmare. She'd had it many times. But she'd thought the dark man was Hunter…maybe it was.

Her body shook with the effort of dragging her attention back to the battle taking place between the two men.

"Think about it, Hunter," Viktor urged. "You know who it is. He was one of yours."

In a move so fast Rowen had to blink just to be sure she'd seen it, Hunter wrapped the fingers of his right hand around Viktor's throat and practically lifted him off the floor.

"Liar," he growled savagely. "I knew my men. They're all dead."

What the hell was he talking about?

Before she could think about what she was doing, Rowen had marched straight up to the two and grabbed hold of Hunter's sleeve. "Don't," she pleaded.

Ten seconds passed before he relented and released Viktor. He turned what she presumed to be a glare beneath those concealing shades in her direction.

"Back off," he ordered gruffly.

"You back off." She stepped even closer, putting herself directly between the two men. "This isn't solving anything. As interesting as watching you two go at each other is, I don't have the time to waste." She turned to Viktor. "If you know something, tell me what it is and drop the riddles."

Viktor smiled again. This time, it lacked the malice of the last time. "She's a fiery one, Hunter. I should have taken her when I had the chance."

Had Rowen not been standing between them, Hunter would have gone for his throat again. As it was, the tension of restraining himself radiated off him in palpable waves.

"Answer me, Azariel," she demanded. "What do you know about these murders?"

"Hunter should be the one to tell you," he said cagily.

"I'm asking you," she pushed, determined not to be distracted by his games.

Viktor reached up. Rowen defied the urge to draw away. She would not allow him to see her fear. He touched her hair, then trailed his fingers along her throat. She trembled, but refused to let him see how his touch got to her.

"I watched you with him," Viktor said, his voice somehow more compelling than usual. Alluring. "I envied him. Wanted you for myself." He shrugged. "Couldn't help myself. After all—" he glanced from her to Hunter "—it's only human to covet what thy brother possesses."

Rowen felt Hunter stiffen behind her.

"Get to the point," she snapped, fed up with the tension vibrating all around her.

"I decided to take you." Viktor licked his lips. She couldn't help feeling violated somehow by the movement…as if he'd touched her with that viperous tongue. "You won't remember that night."

Rowen felt trepidation thread its way through her. He had to be lying. She'd never met him before coming to his house after his call. And she damned sure had no business feeling any sort of attraction to him.

"Hunter intervened—in a sense took your place."

The muscles of her throat worked with the need to swallow, but it proved impossible. She didn't want to believe his words…didn't want to go where this was headed.

"I could have killed him that night," Viktor said gently, "and he could have done the same to me, but fate had other plans and we both survived." His gaze shifted to Hunter once more before he continued. "But that night, that commingling of blood made us the same. *Brothers.*"

The full implication of what his words meant sent her emotions staggering. She braced herself against the dizziness as she turned to Hunter. "Is he telling the truth?"

Without taking his attention off the man he obviously considered his enemy, he answered, "He's telling his version of the truth."

"What does this have to do with the South End Murders?" This she directed to Viktor, since he appeared more inclined to talk than Hunter.

"Ask Hunter about his team," Viktor suggested.

"They're all dead," Hunter snarled. "All of them."

Rowen held her breath, sensed that the revelations to come would change everything.

"No," Viktor argued fiercely. "You felt his presence just as I did. Even with the drugs, you knew it was him. He's here, waiting in that place we once knew."

"Impossible."

"He's here. He's brought us all here together for one purpose."

"What purpose is that?" Hunter demanded, unconvinced.

"To destroy the only ones who can destroy him."

"We're wasting our time." Hunter put his hand on Rowen's arm. "Let's go."

As he ushered her to the door, Viktor called out to him, "Mark my words, Hunter."

Hunter paused to look back at him. Rowen did the same. In that infinitesimal moment before Viktor spoke, Rowen felt her world shift. Understood unequivocally that this enigmatic man, either by cooperation or merely by comprehension of the events to come, represented some inexplicable threat to her existence.

"The woman is next."

Chapter Ten

Rowen kept quiet all the way back into Boston. She'd ordered Hunter to take her home where she could change and pick up her Glock. He'd agreed without argument.

She made a quick call to Merv to bring him up to speed on her whereabouts and offered him a fabricated explanation of where she'd been earlier that morning when he'd first tried to reach her.

Lying to your partner was a cardinal sin in her line of work, and she knew it better than anyone. She would owe Merv a huge accounting when this was over.

Assuming she survived.

The woman is next.

The message written in Finch's blood on that white sheet made her shudder even though the water spraying down on her was as hot as she could tolerate.

Rowen wasn't sure she would ever be warm again.

How had Viktor Azariel known about the message? She refused to believe he had any sort of psychic powers; but then again, it wasn't entirely outside the boundaries of reason. She couldn't say she didn't acknowledge that heightened senses, ESP and the like, existed. She just hesitated to lend any credence to the man's whole bizarre way of life.

He'd said he had envied Hunter...had wanted her for himself. A quivery sensation went through her and her nipples pebbled. Her fingers trailed down and over her breasts, and she closed her eyes as they tingled from her touch. She thought of Hunter and all they'd shared before. She'd only made love once since her time with him. That one time had been a mistake and had left her feeling empty and disillusioned. So she'd thrown herself into work. Had sentenced his memory to her dreams and there he'd stayed...until now.

How could he come back after all this time, after what he'd done to her, and make her feel this way?

Her eyes flew open as she considered that perhaps it was Viktor who turned her on so irrationally. No. She forced her mind away from that scenario.

He could be part of this, for all she knew. In reality, he was involved on some level.

Whether or not he was a good guy, totally twisted in any case, she couldn't say.

Forcing herself to go through the cleansing rituals, she contemplated the sound judgment of leaving Hunter alone downstairs. He could be gone when she went in search of him, following up on the suggestion that one of his old team members was the murderer in this case.

But she doubted he would leave. His need to protect her appeared to override all else.

She just didn't understand his motivation. If he hadn't cared enough about her to stay three years ago, why would he care if she lived or died now?

Maybe she wanted to believe he regretted that long-ago decision, but that was really stupid. She was thirty-one. Fantasies were for teenagers still writhing in puberty. She was too smart to do this to herself anymore.

But she wanted to. As if to punctuate the epiphany, her body pulsated with need. Every part of her, she realized as she moved the soap over her skin, felt heavy and achy. She didn't like feeling this way.

Finch was dead, she reminded herself. So were Ellen Green and Carlotta Simpson. She mentally ticked off the names of the other three victims. She didn't have time to be thinking about her own selfish desires right now. Nailing this killer had to be her one goal.

Nothing else could get in the way.

Not even Hunter.

After emerging from the shower, she patted her skin dry and made fast work of blow-drying her hair. Time was wasting. Every second she spent on anything else was one she could have focused on the case.

Wearing navy slacks and a matching blazer, along with a white blouse and comfortable flats, she finally felt presentable. She'd pulled on her shoulder holster and nestled her Glock where it belonged.

Generally she wore her hair in a serviceable bun or

French twist. But she hadn't bothered this morning, so it hung down her back. She refused to consider that the hairstyle had been an unconscious choice to please Hunter. He'd always liked her hair down.

When she moved down the stairs, she found him poring over a local map.

"Have you found something?" The smell of fresh-brewed coffee wafted from the kitchen and, even before he answered, she'd started in that direction.

"I'm not sure."

Frowning, Rowen poured herself a much needed cup of coffee and rummaged for a breakfast bar. She tried to recall Viktor's words to Hunter—*in that place we once knew.*

That had to mean something specific to Hunter.

Maybe he was holding out on her.

Rowen returned to the parlor where he sat at her desk, hunched over the map. She walked over and looked over his shoulder. *Boston Harbor.* The islands?

"You and Viktor shared an adventure on one of the islands?" she guessed.

"We did."

She sipped her coffee in an attempt to slow her temper, then said, "Can you be more specific?"

He didn't look up. "It's complicated."

"You know what?" Rowen set her coffee mug on the closest table and tossed her breakfast bar next to it. Hunter looked up this time. "I'm out of here," she said flatly. "I have a series of murders to solve. I don't have time to play twenty questions with you, Hunter."

"Give me five minutes, *Rowen*."

Where had she heard that before? And why the hell did her insides quiver every damned time he said her name?

She heaved out a disgusted sigh. "I don't know, Hunter. I'm reasonably sure I've already risked my shield by allowing you at that crime scene this morning. Five more minutes might be more than I can spare. A cop is dead. This city is in a panic." Every station she'd scanned on the radio as Hunter had driven across town had been reporting the danger of citizens going out of their homes at night. The danger was real. Even the police weren't safe, the announcers urged.

Hunter stood, pointed to the map on her desk. "Gallops Island," he said, as if that should mean something to her.

She knew better than this. "What about it?"

"Viktor and his followers used to call the island home."

That couldn't be right. Rowen searched her memory banks. "Wait. That island was closed years ago." She mentioned the year, recalled quite clearly reading about it. "Asbestos or something. The contamination was related to military use." She remembered reading about it in the *Reporter,* of all places.

"That's what the government wanted people to believe."

She let him see her skepticism. "What are you saying?"

"I'm saying that Viktor and his followers were red

flagged by the Bureau. A team was sent there five years ago and reportedly found nothing. But when the incidents continued, another team was called in two years later."

Three years ago, when she'd met Hunter. He and his team had come to Boston to research whatever it was they researched. She'd had a vague idea. Psychic phenomena. He'd kept his work to himself and she hadn't asked. She knew all about security classifications and she didn't have authorization to know what his work consisted of. It wasn't a problem…until he walked away and never looked back.

Resentment scorched through her. She tried. She really tried not to go there, but it was impossible. Dammit, she still had feelings for the man. How totally stupid was that? But she couldn't let him inside again. Couldn't let him do what he'd done before, take her heart into his hands and then walk away.

"What kind of incidents?" She set her hands on her hips and gave him a look that summed up her position.

"At first, it was dead rabbits. Dozens and dozens of dead rabbits washing up on other shores."

Rabbits? She remembered reading in that same *Reporter* article that the island's major population consisted of rabbits. Lots and lots of rabbits.

Realization hit her then. "Viktor and his friends," she guessed. She suppressed a shudder at the idea.

"Nobody really worried about the rabbits, but before long there was a body or two, then ten, and that was a different story."

She shook her head. "That's impossible. If there were murders I would have known about it. That's our jurisdiction."

"Technically, it's the Bureau's—former military post. We took over control from the Massachusetts Department of Conservation and Recreation years ago."

"A military post? Hunter, that's ancient history. World War II or something like that."

"Civil War, as well. Soldiers were quartered there back then."

She held up her hands, her patience at an end. "All right. So Viktor and his crowd had inhabited Gallops Island. They used the wildlife for survival. I suppose that's no different from those who hunt deer on the mainland."

Hunter stared at the floor a moment, then, to her surprise, he reached up and took off his dark glasses so that he could look directly at her. He blinked a couple of times and then those gray eyes bored into hers like twin laser beams. "That's one way to look at it."

Her hackles rose. Had he considered her rationalization a way of siding with Viktor? That was hardly what she'd intended.

"What's your way of looking at it?" she asked sharply.

"Viktor Azariel came here from Eastern Europe. He amassed untold wealth in less than a decade. While his followers survived on the wildlife of Gallops Island, he erected a mansion in the Berkshires."

Wasn't that, too, the way the world worked? The few

grew rich and fat, so to speak, while most slaved for a pittance, barely getting by. The system worked the same in most cultures.

"So, he's a jerk. Did he gain his wealth through illegal means?" She didn't doubt that for a second. He seemed exactly the type.

"No. He's legit in his business dealings."

"Look." She glanced at her watch. She really had to get out of here. "Just cut to the chase, Hunter. I'm late." When she'd made an appearance at the office, she wanted to check in on Finch's autopsy.

That piercing gaze leveled on hers, seeming to look right into her thoughts. She shifted uneasily.

"When my team came in, we had certain orders," Hunter told her. "We learned that the original team hadn't reported accurately, but no one ever owned up to the discrepancy. Due to the nature of the situation, we were to analyze the circumstances and then the whole population was to be exterminated."

His words stunned her. *Exterminated.* These were people he was talking about. "Are you serious?"

He nodded. "Viktor is different on some level. His *kind* carries an unexplained gene. Something the scientific world can't account for. Personally, I believe it falls into the category of a hereditary mutation, but my opinion isn't the final say."

A picture had begun to form in her head. "This mutated gene creates this disease—the need for constant transfusions of fresh blood?"

"Yes. A thirst, Viktor calls it."

Rowen closed her eyes for a second and held up both hands. "Okay. So he claims that this whatever it is makes him a vampire?" Even as she said the words, she wanted to take them back.

"That's right. He claims he was there on Gallops Island before the Mass 54th Regiment."

The air rushed out of her lungs. A pre-Civil War vampire, no less. "Right. So, how were his *kind* exterminated? Stakes through the heart?" They were way, way into that creepy zone now. Laughter bubbled up in her throat. Unfortunately, it wasn't from amusement; it was more like hysteria. This was too much for a common, everyday cop to absorb.

"They were executed, then burned."

She blinked. He was serious. "How can that be? They were human…right?"

Hunter dropped his head. "There were those who didn't think so."

Another reality took her breath. "You were in charge of this…this massacre?" Oh, God. Surely Hunter wouldn't have gone along with anything like that.

"No. I didn't know in the beginning what was planned. I was a scientist. But my confirmation of the threat is what initiated the action. When I found out, I tried to stop it but I was too late."

"So, they all died?"

"All but Viktor and a handful of his closest followers."

"You warned him…that's why he didn't kill you that

night." Viktor had said he could have killed Hunter, but he hadn't. Fate had had other plans for them. This couldn't be real. Too off the wall. "Hunter, I'm not sure—"

"I know what you think." He rubbed at his eyes and she wondered if going without the shielding glasses was too much for him. The room was barely lit. The blinds closed tightly, but that still might exceed his tolerance. "My team conducted research which addressed phenomena beyond the normal range of what is scientifically explainable."

She got that. Telekinesis, telepathy, precognition, clairvoyance, the works, including spirits and other lifeforms. But he was a scientist, not a regular agent. To stand by and watch the execution of any life-form, human or not, had to have gone against the grain of all that he believed.

"So Viktor and a small number escaped and you pretended not to notice."

"Yes."

Her head ached. Rowen rubbed her temples with her thumb and forefinger. "What does this have to do with the South End Murders?" A part of her didn't want to know this. Like most, she required a certain level of optimism and faith in mankind in general to survive. Even seven years as a cop hadn't jaded her that badly.

"I warned Viktor that he should look for alternative methods to fulfill his needs. A way that wouldn't draw attention to him or his followers."

The donor system. But that wasn't anything new.

Certainly not within the past three years. This was an old cult system.

"He adopted a method he insisted some of his kind had used for centuries."

Well, that clarified that issue. "That still doesn't answer the basic question." Though she found Viktor's history intriguing, she had bigger problems just now. "Who is committing these murders?"

"Whoever it is knows about Viktor." Hunter moved around the desk, came closer to her. "He knows I allowed some to escape three years ago."

Another frown tugged at her brow. "But you said your entire team was killed."

"They were. There's no question there."

"Then how can Viktor be right about that? And if he's not, what does this have to do with you or me?"

"The first team. The ones who claimed they found nothing. It has to be someone involved with that team."

"Does Viktor believe the first team found something?" She still didn't see how it fit, but somehow it started to lean in that direction, had her instincts humming. "If they didn't find anything, how would they know?"

Hunter gestured to her computer. "I've gone into the Bureau's database and reviewed the records of the six members of that first team."

She raised an eyebrow in question. "How can you do that? You're not with the Bureau anymore."

"I know a couple of back doors."

The idea that he stood only a couple of feet away suddenly bothered her…made her too ill at ease in her own skin. "What did you find?"

"Three are dead. One works in private practice, one has advanced up the ranks at the Bureau's Washington division. But the final one, the one who would have been in charge, left the Bureau four years ago. Just six months after his team assessed the Gallops Island incident."

"All right. I'm with you so far."

"It's as if he dropped off the face of the earth after that."

That in itself would be suspicious. "The Bureau hasn't kept track of him? Isn't that standard protocol?"

"It is. But he's somehow fallen through the net."

"What's his name?"

"Nathan McGill. No wife, no kids, just one sister: Marge *Finch.* Your dead cop was McGill's nephew."

ROWEN STRODE THROUGH the marble-floored lobby of One Schroeder Plaza and boarded a waiting elevator. At this time of morning, one didn't have to wait.

She didn't slow down until she'd reached the chief's office and even then, she ignored his secretary as she tried to waylay Rowen.

The chief looked up as she burst into his private sanctuary. From the looks of his two visitors, only one of whom was familiar to Rowen, they hadn't expected any interruptions. The one man she recognized was on the city planning board. Considering his presence, they were likely discussing expansion or upgrading of facilities.

"We have to talk."

Chief Koppel looked from Rowen to the two men. "Will you excuse me, gentlemen?" Apparently he understood that what she had to say couldn't wait.

The two got up and left the room, eyeing her speculatively as they did.

"Detective O'Connor, you'd better have a damned good reason for this intrusion." He gestured for her to take a chair. "You're already on my shit list. We had to conduct a press conference, as well as briefing the mayor, without you this morning and you're the lead investigator on this case."

She sat down reluctantly, fighting back the fury and attempting to escape her flimsy hold on composure. "Why was Detective Finch assigned to my case?"

A frown furrowed across the chief's broad forehead. "What the hell are you talking about? He just transferred in. Why wouldn't I assign him to the hottest case on the books?"

Not outside the realm of possibility.

"No one asked you to assign him to our group?"

A flicker of something like surprise flashed in his eyes before he could stop it. "Why do you ask?"

"Just tell me the truth, Chief. Did someone ask you to assign Finch to this case?"

He shrugged. "The mayor's personal assistant. The mayor is apparently an old friend of his mother's. You know she's the only family Finch had," he added as an aside. "The mayor's assistant passed along the request. Finch wanted to make a big splash. We needed the manpower. That's where I would have put him anyway."

Well, Finch had sure as hell gotten his big splash. Unfortunately, there wouldn't be any encores. "Do you know Finch's mother?"

Chief Koppel shook his head. "What the hell is this about, O'Connor?"

"Finch was set up," she told him. "He was supposed to die. It was a warning to me."

She'd had to swear on her life that she wouldn't tell anything Hunter had told her. He waited close by. He wouldn't say where, just said he'd be watching her. But she had to know that the chief was not in on this. It was crazy. Because they didn't have a suspect, everyone suddenly was one. For her own piece of mind, whatever the hell was going on, she had to be sure the chief was with her.

Koppel leaned forward, braced his arms on his desk. "Look, O'Connor, this case is getting to all of us, but I think maybe you're taking this the wrong way. You can't be sure the message was about you. Four other female victims have died. The message could be for any female walking the streets of Boston. Why don't you track down Merv and the two of you can hash this out." He sighed. "I have a meeting with the Bureau this afternoon. They're going to send in one of their special teams."

She shook her head, almost laughed. Too little, too late. "They won't find anything, Chief. This isn't about the murders. It's about something bigger…I just haven't figured out what yet."

He let go a mighty breath. "Do me a favor, O'Connor. When you figure it out, let me in on it, would you?"

She walked out of his office, confident that he was innocent of any involvement. But the mayor or his personal assistant was a different story. One or both of them had placed Finch in her investigation for some reason other than for him to make a big splash, as the chief had called it.

Rowen made a quick call to Merv and the two of them rendezvoused at their favorite coffeehouse. To Rowen's dismay, he brought Doherty with him. She wasn't sure about trusting the other detective but at this point, time was too short not to. Besides, Merv probably felt more as if Doherty was his partner these days.

"You're sure about this," Merv ventured.

She'd told him the parts Hunter had said were safe to pass along. Bureau connection. Agent turned bad guy, etc.

"I'm certain."

"Why would the guy want to set up his own nephew?" Doherty wanted to know.

She couldn't answer that one. But she would get to the truth. Maybe he hadn't. Maybe Finch was supposed to keep someone abreast of the investigation. Some of Viktor's people could have done this despite his denial.

"I need you and Doherty to keep an eye on the mayor and his assistant. Do a little unofficial eavesdropping."

"You want us to put the mayor and his personal assistant under surveillance?" Doherty's eyes were wide with disbelief as he asked the question. He surely thought she'd lost her mind, and maybe she had.

"That's right."

"You know what you're asking is illegal, don't you, Ro?"

The eavesdropping. "Yes, I do. I'm lead investigator. I'll take the rap if you get caught."

Merv shrugged. "All right, then. So what're you going to be doing in the meantime?"

She needed to see Cost and then she intended to find Nathan McGill. "I'll check in with Cost and work on finding Finch's missing uncle."

If Doherty couldn't be trusted, she was in real trouble here. Her gaze must have shifted to him as she considered whether or not the detective was trustworthy because he spoke up.

"I know you don't trust me," he said. "Not like you do Merv here. But you can count on me. I've never let a partner down yet."

Rowen wondered if when this was all said and done she would be able to say the same. She'd lied to her partner at least twice. Would likely lie to him again before this was over.

But there was no other way, not if she intended to keep Viktor Azariel's secret.

The question was, did Azariel's conclusions justify the risk she was taking?

"Good. Merv and I need you."

When she was about to leave the coffeehouse, Merv held her up outside the ladies' room. "You sure you're okay, Ro? You look exhausted."

She squeezed his arm. "We're all exhausted, Merv. But we're going to figure this out."

He nodded. "Doherty and I will take care of the mayoral connection. You just take care of you."

"Don't worry about me, I've got my own personal guardian angel."

His eyebrows winged upward. "The guy in black from the crime scene this morning?"

She nodded.

"He definitely looks like he could play the part."

Her cell phone rang just then. "I'll touch base with you later. Give me a call if you learn anything useful."

Merv gave her a nod and sauntered off to catch up with Doherty.

Both men were putting their careers in her hands. She hoped like hell she wouldn't let them down.

"O'Connor."

"Detective, I have something for you."

The M.E.

"Give me something good, Doc, I'm getting desperate here." Rowen leaned her forehead against the wall and listened, hoping against hope this would be the break she needed.

"I found the drug."

Her head came up. "Give me the details, Doc. Don't leave anything out."

ROWEN DROVE BACK to her place shortly after 2 p.m. Hunter would be on her tail somewhere, but he was good. She hadn't seen him. But he was there…she could feel him.

She parked, unlocked her door and went inside. This confrontation had to be conducted on her turf. Cost had given her the one thing she needed most.

The weapon the killer used to render his victims helpless.

Out of habit, she filled the polka-dot bowls. Princess came into the kitchen to check out what Rowen was up to. She sniffed, turned up her nose and went back to her cushion.

"Finicky mutt," she grumbled.

If she didn't love the hell out of Princess, she'd donate the dog to some kid who had nothing better to do than cater to the spoiled pooch. But she loved Princess too much to even think about it.

She heard the knob turn on the back door and she unholstered her Glock.

With a few turns and clicks of his lock pick, Hunter had the door open. Lowering her weapon, she said, "You couldn't just knock?"

"The sound," he told her. He gestured to his ears.

She nodded. Oh yeah. She'd forgotten about that. He did look tense. "Are you taking your medicine?" He'd said the medicine helped him to cope, but there were side effects.

"Let's not talk about me. What did you learn?"

She gave him a quick rundown on her meeting with Merv and Doherty. He'd already known that phase of her plan.

"Cost?"

His clipped question made her worry that the medication wasn't working effectively, but as he said, this wasn't about him. This was about the case and six murders.

"Have you ever heard of Pavulon?"

"Yes."

Another short answer, the tension behind the single word undeniable.

"Okay, the drug Cost found in Finch's body works very similar to Pavulon. It's a neuromuscular transmission interrupter. Almost instantly renders victims completely paralyzed and mute. You have to be testing specifically for it to find it, and after about twelve hours it becomes undetectable. The really sick part is that the victim is fully aware of what's happening to him or her until the last beat of his heart."

"That's why none of the victims put up a struggle."

She nodded. "He used a really small-gauge needle. Extremely hard to find unless you're looking specifically for it. When the tox screens came up clean, there was no reason to do an in-depth inspection of the bodies in search of a needle prick. The usual examination yielded nothing."

His silence indicated he was mulling over the new information, but Rowen had already had a chance to do just that.

"The kicker," she went on, "is that the drug was developed by Azariel's pharmaceutical company. It's supposedly the hottest new painkiller on the market. For use in extreme cases."

Hunter regarded her long enough for her fury to ignite.

"I'm telling you he's involved," she clarified just in case he didn't get it.

Hunter shook his head. "Why would he set himself up that way? Think about it, *Rowen.* The drug would lead right back to him. Perhaps that is what someone wants."

She let go a breath of total exhaustion. He was right. She was looking for an easy answer and it wasn't there.

"So this murderer is a normal human, not Viktor or one of his kind." She couldn't believe she'd made a distinction between Viktor's kind and normal humans, but there it was. "But why would some ex-Bureau agent start playing vampire to draw us all into this little game?"

"I've been doing some research of my own," he said bluntly. "A training facility once stood on Gallops Island. I think it was used by the military ages ago, but it eventually fell into ruins. According to what I've found, there has been a great deal of activity the past two years back and forth out to the island. So-called cleanup efforts, but I know that's a sham. The contamination was a cover-up."

"But it was closed years ago. Its inhabitants exterminated," she reminded. "What's left?"

"Exactly. Something has been going on out there."

"And we have to find out what?" she suggested. It might not have anything to do with their case, but Viktor seemed to think it did. He'd told Hunter to go back to where they had once been. Bottom line—it was all they had. Knowing all that, a part of her still wanted to believe Viktor was involved somehow.

"*I* have to find out what," Hunter corrected. "You're staying out of this part. It's Bureau business."

"Like hell." She went toe-to-toe with him. "You're not leaving me out of this, Hunter. Don't even think about it. You try and I'll tell the chief everything. Besides, you're not Bureau, either, remember?"

Six Boston citizens were dead, one being a cop. No way was she backing off.

"If my assumptions are correct and we're discovered, we're dead."

"All the more reason you need backup."

He reached for her with one gloved hand. Traced the line of her cheek making her shiver. "I don't want you to get caught in the cross fire," he murmured.

"Too late. I've already been targeted, remember?"

There was nothing he could say to that. He knew she was right. No matter what he did, she was in this.

"So," she suggested, taking a mental step back to relieve some of the tension, "do you have a plan?"

"We need the cover of darkness."

Sounded reasonable to her. "Then we wait?"

"We wait."

Chapter Eleven

Evan wrestled with the decision for two hours before he made the call. Rowen had spent most of that same time in deep discussion with her partner and the other detective working the South End Murders. She'd brought them up to speed on the drug the M.E. had found, but she'd kept quiet about the other. So far, neither the mayor nor his assistant had made any covert moves.

Evan felt confident no one in the mayor's office was really involved. The request to see that Finch was assigned to the investigation had somehow come from his uncle. Hunter doubted this case was anywhere near that complicated, and yet it was immensely so.

In fact, he had reasoned that it was utterly simple and literally ingenious. That was the reason he'd dared to call his old field supervisor.

It had been nearly three years since he'd spoken to the man and Evan found it difficult to do so now, but it was necessary.

He went into the darkest room of the house and gave

himself ample time to brace for the coming sensory overload. The medication had grown all but impotent in the past twenty-four hours. He had to make the most of what time remained; he had very little of the precious commodity left. He knew the signs—he was headed for a complete breakdown.

When Special Supervisory Agent Wesley Braham came on the line, Evan didn't bother with small talk. "What do you know about Nathan McGill and his current activities?"

The silence on the other end of the line sent a new wave of tension through Evan. He closed his eyes against the pain that followed.

"He disappeared," Braham admitted. "Just dropped off the face of the planet, like he never existed."

That was it? Nothing? Evan's eyes narrowed with suspicion. "It's difficult for me to believe that the agency has no idea what became of him," Evan countered.

"Believe me, Hunter. If we could find him, don't think we wouldn't. We want him something bad."

"I take it that means he left on less than favorable terms." Evan needed more than the fact that the man had dropped off the planet. He had known about his abrupt departure; he just didn't know the circumstances.

"Why the questions about McGill? What are you up to, Hunter?"

"I was bored," he deadpanned. "I needed something to pass the time, so I thought I'd look into missing agents."

Another moment of silence passed.

"Does this mean the medication is working?"

Evan closed his eyes and grappled for patience. "This isn't about me, Braham." He shouldn't be surprised that the man would ask. He'd been the one who waited day and night in the hospital until Evan had awakened. He'd been there for him during the attempt at rehab and then the final decision to go into seclusion. Braham had been a good friend, but he was a part of a life that no longer existed for Evan. He had to keep that in mind. Couldn't get too close…not even to Rowen.

"According to the trace I put on this call, you're calling from Boston."

Evan had expected as much.

"What's in Boston, Hunter? The woman you left behind or the case?"

"Just give me what I need, Braham." A dull ache had started in his forehead. Too many stimuli. He needed to rest. He needed quiet…darkness. Viktor's accusation echoed in his brain. Outside the healing, there was only one cure for what ailed him…*death*.

Every instinct warned Evan that that time was very close at hand for him. On many levels, it would be a relief. His mind turned back a page and focused on Rowen. Leaving her again would be his only regret.

"We suspected he'd been selling out the Gateway Program," Braham said bluntly. "We couldn't prove it but his abrupt disappearance speaks for itself."

"The program as in information," Evan asked, his gut

telling him this was far worse than the manipulation of data for profit, "or the people?"

Most of the cases Gateway had investigated had turned out to be hoaxes. But, occasionally, there was the real thing…true phenomenon. The rare human being who possessed a special gift or peculiar genetic trait.

"Maybe both," Braham confirmed grimly. "He was so damned good at deception we haven't been able to even get close to finding him. Undoubtedly he's taken a whole new identity by now. Hell, he could be anyone, anywhere."

Not anywhere, Evan mused. McGill was here in Boston. The only real question was why.

Evan thanked his old friend and carefully avoided additional questions. Braham didn't like being left out of the loop, but he needed to keep in mind that Evan no longer worked for the Bureau. He answered to no one except himself.

He knew exactly what he had to do.

ROWEN SPREAD THE PICTURES and her notes over the kitchen table and studied what she'd learned. Not much. Merv had called her back with the latest on his surveillance of Mayor Dwight Schmale and his assistant, Lionel Campbell. Not the first thing out of the ordinary. Both had left the office around five thirty, each had gone to his respective home. Doherty had the assistant's Bay Village row house under observation; claiming seniority Merv covered the mayor's Beacon Hill residence.

She had a feeling, a gut instinct, quietly building up momentum against that lead. It was going to be another dead end. But they had to pursue every single lead. A long-distance interview of Finch's mother had revealed nothing. He worked hard, played even harder, but nothing else. No steady girlfriend, no affiliation with clubs, or even a church, for that matter. He'd recently applied to one of the local universities to go after his MBA in finance. The man obviously had higher aspirations than spending the rest of his life dredging up clues related to dead bodies. The mother hadn't heard from Finch's one other relative, Nathan McGill, in more than five years. She thought he was dead.

Rowen knew that feeling. She had believed Hunter dead for three years.

The faces of the victims stared up at Rowen, and desolation welled inside her. None of them were connected, with the exception of the two tattooed victims. They didn't run in the same circles; their financial statuses were all different; there was no relevance in age. Absolutely nothing. And, yet, somehow, they were all linked to the same madman.

Her thoughts drifted upstairs and to the man resting in the darkness. He was convinced Viktor was not responsible. And even she had to admit that the drug would have been a stupid move. It definitely fit more in line with a setup.

Whatever this was, whoever had taken these lives,

had brought the three of them together. Rowen, Hunter and Viktor. That part she was certain of. An unholy trinity at worst, an unlikely alliance at best—a burned-out, damaged FBI agent, a desperate cop with baggage of her own and a frigging self-proclaimed vampire. Her head moved from side to side in resignation. What a team.

But she sensed deep inside that she couldn't finish this without those two men. She thought back to that last time she'd gone to Viktor's home alone. She wished she could remember what had happened during those missing hours, but there was nothing. He made her feel things; there was no question about that. Not the same kind of feelings she experienced for Hunter. Viktor's lure was about dark temptation, delving into the forbidden.

Unfortunately for her, she still cared for Hunter, on a much deeper level than merely the physical.

She swiped her palms on her slacks and told herself not to go down this road just now, but she had to. What if they didn't survive the night? She needed to consider her feelings and make peace with him before…well, before this was over. Holding a grudge these past three years had been a heavy burden. She hated the bitterness and the hurt that went along with it. It was past time to let it go. She might not be able to forgive him, but what was the point in wasting energy hating him when she knew deep down she never truly would?

He'd told her that his decision not to come back to

Boston—to her—had been made before his accident. She could deal with that. She was an adult. She'd had three years to come to terms with the idea that he hadn't felt the same way she did. Their time together apparently had not affected him the way it had her. How could she hold that against him? He'd broken her heart, that was true. But maybe his work had dictated a life of staying focused and unattached. He had been thirty-three when they were together. She should have taken that into consideration. If he'd been the marrying kind, or even the commitment type, he would surely had done so by then. She just hadn't wanted to see it.

So it was her fault her heart had gotten broken, right?

Rowen rolled her eyes and cursed herself. Why was it a woman always looked for ways to blame whatever had gone wrong in a relationship on herself?

She hadn't done anything wrong. The only thing she was guilty of was trusting the man who'd made her fall in love with him.

Okay, enough with that. There was no rationalizing what happened between them. She could stir it around and view the circumstances from different angles all she wanted; the end result would be the same. He'd walked away, and she'd paid the price.

She closed her eyes and refused to dwell on how harshly fate had dealt with him. It was a miracle he'd survived, and he paid dearly for that survival every minute of every day. Judging by his reaction to little things, like that breaking cup or her slugging him—okay, maybe that was a big thing—he suffered a great deal. Light, sound, touch, smell—all of it burdened him.

She wondered how he lived at all.

Maybe he didn't.

There she went feeling sorry for him again.

They did need to talk.

To resolve their issues and get on with their lives, assuming they lived through this night.

Determined to follow her instincts, or maybe her foolish heart, Rowen trudged into the entry hall and up the stairs before she could change her mind.

It would be dark soon and moving forward with their plan would take precedence. Having this talk had to be now or never.

She paused outside her bedroom. She should have suggested he take the guest room, but hers was the only one with an en suite bath. Just another example of not thinking the situation all the way through. But then again, it wasn't as if they hadn't ever shared her bed.

Whatever. Get this over with. She started to raise her fist to knock, then remembered that would be too harsh. Leaning closer to the door, she held her breath and listened. Silence. He could be sleeping.

No way. Not Hunter. He might rest his eyes and his mind from sights and sounds and smells, but he wouldn't go to sleep. Not at a time like this.

Turning the knob slowly so as to limit any squeaking it might do, she opened the door very slowly. She hadn't turned on the hallway light, so the room remained in darkness as she moved inside. She blinked to adjust, but couldn't see a thing. The outline of the bed formed in her mind but that could very well be simply because she knew where it was.

Moving deeper into the room, she held out her hands to prevent herself from bumping into anything. At the bed, she touched the covers lightly. She didn't want to startle him. No worry. He wasn't there.

The bed was empty, as least as far as she could reach from the side where she stood.

Fury rocketed through her.

If he'd sneaked away without her…

Dammit. She should never have trusted him.

She reached for the lamp on the bedside and clicked it on. A soft golden glow spilled over the bedside table and the rumpled linens of the bed.

No sign of Hunter.

She swore, cursed herself for being an idiot.

Just then, something in her peripheral vision caught her attention. Black…

She turned to get a better look and recognized Hunter's long coat lying across the bench positioned at the foot of the bed. Her gaze moved from there to the dresser, where his dark glasses lay.

He wouldn't leave without those.

"What's wrong?"

She whirled around so fast her eyes needed a moment to focus. Hunter stood in the doorway of the en suite bath. He held up one hand to block the dim light from the lamp. His hair was wet and hanging around his shoulders. Then the towel hanging around his lean hips registered with her.

"Sorry, I didn't realize you were…" She gestured awkwardly to the bathroom.

"Do you mind throwing my shirt over the lamp?" He pointed to the clothes he'd left on the floor on the other side of the room. "It'll filter out some of the glare."

Rowen hurried to do as he asked. And he was right. The black fabric of his shirt dimmed the lamp's illumination considerably, leaving the room mostly in shadows. That done, she stood there, feeling suddenly out of place in her own home.

"You wanted to talk?" he asked when she couldn't seem to find her voice.

She stared at the covered lamp, thinking that she'd been too hasty in her decision to come into the room like this.

He'd moved up behind her…too close. She could smell the soft clean scent of his skin and the soap he'd used. The idea that he was naked save for the towel affected her more than it should have.

"I talked to Merv," she said without turning around. "Still nothing on the mayor or the assistant. I'm beginning to think that's another dead end."

"I agree."

She couldn't stand here with her back to him forever. Eventually she had to turn around, or he would know that she dreaded the full frontal encounter. And, God, she did. More than likely, he already sensed her trepidation. He read her entirely too well.

Steeling herself, she pivoted and looked up into his unshielded face. "How much longer do you suppose we should wait before we get started?" Dusk had begun to settle; a heavy blanket of darkness would follow. The cloud cover would ensure that there would be no light from the stars and perhaps even the moon. Spending too much time in the dark with Hunter was beginning to make her doubt her ability to remain objective where he was concerned, which meant this setting in particular was not a good idea.

Case in point: the way his gray eyes seemed to capture the sparse light and sparkle with it. Or the way the shadows played over the angles and planes of his handsome face. She'd dreamed of him, ached for him so many nights. It just wasn't fair to be here with him like this now and not be able to touch him.

"Not much longer now," he murmured, his gaze dropping to her lips as he spoke. "We need the cover of total darkness."

She licked her lips, bit down on the lower one to prevent the trembling that had started there. Coming in here like this had been a huge mistake. Why was it she hadn't seen that until now? Her instincts always lagged behind when it came to assessing the threat Hunter presented. "Good," she wrestled out around the lump of uncertainty in her throat. "Let me know when you're ready to go."

There were things she could do, such as change into all-black clothing for stealth, locate her most comfortable and practical shoes for the occasion. She could even load a couple of clips into her utility belt. Anything to occupy the time until then.

She saw his hand reaching for her, but she couldn't get the message from her brain to her body to move. Instead, she stood very, very still and let him touch her. His fingers traced her lips, she shivered, caught her breath.

"I've never forgotten how you taste," he said softly.

This couldn't happen. "Hunter, I—"

He shushed her with those fingers and she watched as he moved closer and closer, leaned down and slowly replaced the touch of his fingers with the brush of his lips.

Something shattered inside her when he kissed her. Something too fragile to survive this moment…to survive him.

His fingers threaded into her hair and he deepened the kiss. She told herself to resist…to fight the need, but she couldn't do anything but get lost in the taste and smell of him…the feel of his lips moving over hers. The temptation of him was too sweet to resist.

He suddenly broke the seal, pressed his forehead against hers, his breath as ragged as if he'd run long and hard. She started to pull away, certain the kiss had been too much for him. She couldn't imagine how he handled the deluge of feelings when it was all she could do herself to bear up.

"Wait," he whispered harshly. "Just give me time."

However badly he'd hurt her three years ago, she couldn't stop the tears that rushed to her eyes. Tears for him, for how he'd suffered…still suffered. Even something as pleasant as the kiss they'd just shared was agony for him. She thought of all the hours they'd spent making love…of how skilled a lover he'd been. This was so unfair.

His fingers tightened where they cradled her head. "Don't waste your time feeling sorry for me," he said roughly. "I'm not beaten yet."

And then he kissed her again. This time, his touch was hard and demanding. Rowen didn't fight him… didn't resist at all. Whoever he was punishing, her or himself, she didn't care. She needed this as much as he seemed to.

With a savage growl, he jerked his lips from hers and moved on to her throat, tasting, teasing, kissing, rushing forward despite the obvious cost. Her head lolled back, giving him full access. Heat shimmered through her, melting every muscle and bone, forcing her to lean into him. Her hands found his bare chest, reveled in the feel of his damp skin as she relearned the man she'd loved what seemed like a lifetime ago now.

He shoved off her jacket and shoulder holster, his movements awkward, brutal. The buttons flew from her blouse as he ripped it from her body. The bra followed, freeing her breasts for his devouring. She whimpered, uncertain she could bear the thrill he incited inside her but craving it. He dragged her to the bed and lowered her there. Her shoes and slacks disappeared, then her panties. The towel fell away from his hips and she arched toward him as he lowered himself onto her. The feel of his weight atop her was like coming home. This was where she belonged…there had never been anyone else who made her feel the way Hunter did.

He kissed her hard, his fingers tangling with hers, restraining her roving hands. She wondered vaguely if her touching him was too much. She felt the press of him against her and she spread her legs in invitation.

Evan held very still, fought to catch his breath with the sensations crashing down on him so hard he couldn't think, much less breathe. He had to slow down, had to stay in control.

She lifted her hips and rubbed intimately against him, and he almost lost his mind. He trembled beneath the onslaught of new sensations. The intensifying pleasure-pain made him light-headed…he couldn't say where the pain ended and the pleasure began. But he couldn't stop. He wanted her more than anything else…even more than his next breath.

Dying in her arms would be worth every second of exquisite agony.

Her fingers plowed into his hair and pulled his mouth down to hers. Her touch vibrated through him, setting him on fire all over again. She kissed him as if her life depended on that one kiss…as if her world would end tomorrow and tonight was all she had.

And maybe it was.

But not if he had anything to do with it.

He plunged inside her and his whole body tensed to the breaking point. His fingers fisted in the sheet. Heat rushed through his veins like liquid fire, made him tremble.

"Hunter," she whispered as her hips began to undulate under his. "Please don't stop now."

His chest was too tight to allow breathing, much less speech. He couldn't respond to her verbally, but he could do as she asked. He moved. The ensuing sensations flooded him, overloading his senses to the point he couldn't think…could barely remain conscious. The feel of her slick, hot body as he thrust in and out, so slowly, so damned slowly, brought tears to his eyes. She pulled him deeper with a strategic arch of her hips, her tight muscles dragging along him creating a mind-blowing friction.

Sweat rose on his skin as he pounded harder, thrust faster, drawing them both toward that elusive peak that might very well kill him.

Her inner muscles contracted. Her entire body tensed and she cried out his name as release claimed her.

His body trembled violently, once, twice, but he didn't stop, didn't slow down. Then his own climax grabbed him by the throat and hurled him into a crash and burn.

Feeling himself erupt inside her was his last conscious thought.

Chapter Twelve

"Hunter!" Fear detonated in her heart.

Rowen's first thought was that she had surely killed him. She should never have allowed him to make love to her. His condition was too unstable…too fragile.

He groaned, reached up to cradle his head.

Thank God. He was moving.

She scrambled off the bed and grabbed a robe. Once she'd knotted the sash around her waist, she climbed back onto the disheveled linens to sit next to him.

"Are you all right?" she asked softly. Her heart pounded so hard she could scarcely hear herself think, but she struggled to keep her voice quiet and calm. She didn't want to add to his agony by becoming hysterical.

"The medicine," he murmured. "Coat pocket."

Rowen reached for the coat, dug through the pockets until she found the prescription bottle. She quickly opened it. "How many?"

"Two."

He sounded weak, his voice reed-thin and shaky. His

hand trembled when she placed the pills there. She bounded off the bed and brought him a glass of water from the bathroom. Careful not to hover, she eased a step away, gave him plenty of breathing room.

"How long will it take for the pills to give you any relief?" Her hand went to her mouth and she tried her level best not to allow the emotions tearing her apart inside to show on the outside. The damage left behind by that explosion had ruined his life. She could see that clearly now. No wonder he'd left the Bureau. Left her…

He managed to heft himself into a sitting position. "It usually works quickly." His head hung between his shoulders as if the strength to hold it up right was too great. His hair fell forward, shielding his face from her view. For a man so strong, this show of weakness had to be extremely difficult for him.

But there was nothing weak about the way he looked otherwise. He still had the same lean, muscular body, the broad shoulders and sculpted torso that made her salivate just looking at him.

"Give me a few moments," he murmured.

She glanced around the room, uncertain whether she should leave him alone or not. "I'll…ah…get dressed."

Rowen gathered clothes and the hiking boots she rarely wore and retreated to the bathroom down the hall. She didn't want to chance that the running water or other sounds she made would aggravate his condition.

For a while, she stood in front of the mirror over the

pedestal sink and stared at herself. How in the world had she let this happen?

He'd shown up in her life after three years, after breaking her heart, and she'd gone and fallen for him again.

"Not the brightest bulb in the chandelier, huh?"

Definitely not.

She spent her days tracking down killers by processing the details she discovered logically and objectively. Why was it she couldn't apply those same techniques to her personal life? The better question was, why Hunter? How could he hold this much power over her?

Shaking her head, she turned on the faucet. Five minutes later she'd washed up and donned her night camouflage. Black jeans, black long-sleeved T-shirt and hiking boots. She bundled her hair on top of her head and shouldered on her holster. All she had to do now was find the wool skullcap she'd had since her college days, when snowboarding and skiing were her favorite pastimes.

Downstairs coat closet, she decided. At least she hoped that's where she'd stored it. She couldn't remember the last time she'd taken off work just to have fun. Too long. That was something else about her life she needed to change.

For now, the case had to be her main focus. The temporary lapse into self-indulgence she and Hunter had just shared couldn't happen again until this case was resolved. And then…

Well, who knew.

Shuffling through the closet, she decided a lightweight black windbreaker would work for concealing her weapon and in case it rained. She found the cap stuffed into a coat pocket. Maybe luck was with her tonight.

Pulling it on, ensuring her hair was stuffed inside it, she elbowed the door closed and started for the stairs. She hoped Hunter was moving around by now. Anticipation had already kicked her heart rate into double time. She wanted to bring down the son of a bitch responsible for six murders.

As noiselessly as possible, she eased open her bedroom door. "Hunter?" she whispered softly.

The table lamp had been turned off, leaving the room pitch-dark. But she didn't have to see to know.

He was gone.

EVAN LOOKED OUT over the Massachusetts Bay. The air was uncannily calm. The rain had stopped and though the cloud cover hid the stars, the moon hung full in the sky, providing ample light but not so much that it pained him.

The boat he'd hired for the night waited near Long Wharf. He glanced toward North Boston as a plane ascended from Logan Airport. The medication had dulled his senses to a tolerable degree, but the peace would not last long.

Making love to Rowen had provided the distraction he needed to give her the slip, but it had taken a significant toll on him.

He gritted his teeth against the emotions that instantly attempted to swell inside him. He would not let this happen a second time. When this was over, if he survived, he would walk away. There was no other option. Rowen deserved the kind of life he was no longer capable of offering.

If protecting her had not been crucial, he would never have returned to Boston or intruded in her life once more. It would have been far better for her to continue believing he was dead.

In reality, he had been dead for three years. The pain was his entire existence. It never really went away. Perhaps if he were not a coward, he would have ended his misery long ago. But, as Viktor said, fate had other plans for him. Fate had brought him back to this place…to *the place he once knew.*

Now he would finish it once and for all.

McGill, or whatever he called himself now, was the only one who remained. The others who'd been a part of the original team who came to investigate Viktor's activities all those years ago knew nothing of his continued existence. To their knowledge, Viktor and his kind had been exterminated. The question now was what part did Viktor play in McGill's entrepreneurial ventures.

Sick bastard. How could a top-notch agent fall victim to temptation? Money. It was the downfall of many.

Evan wasn't entirely sure why McGill had started this, ultimately drawing Viktor, Rowen and Evan himself to this moment. He could only assume it had something to do with Viktor's presence. That was the only connection that tied them all together.

Tonight, he would find out. Every instinct urged him to trust Viktor's assessment that the answer would be found on Gallops Island. The place where Evan and Viktor had first encountered each other.

The beginning of a dangerous liaison.

Evan boarded the boat he'd rented, searched for the keys in the place where the owner had said they would be and prepared to pull out of the slip.

"Put your hands up."

Evan's fingers stilled on the key. All it would take was one flick of the ignition and he could be out of here in a few seconds. She wouldn't shoot. He was certain of that. He'd sensed her feelings for him as she'd come apart in his arms. But she was here… She would only follow him.

He'd thought he would be well away from the shore before she made her way here. He'd taken her car keys, had cut the lines of her phone. But he hadn't been able to locate her cellular. She'd called a cab or her partner.

He slowly turned around, keeping his hands in plain sight. "We both know you won't shoot."

She glared at him. "Maybe you're not as sure as you'd like to be."

One side of his mouth curled into a smile, something he rarely did these days. "Perhaps you have a point."

"You want me to cuff him, Ro? Or maybe I should just shoot him."

Just as Evan had suspected, her partner ambled up

next to her, weapon drawn and aimed directly at him. Of course she would call her partner if she needed backup.

"Well, looks like the gang is all here." They were wasting valuable time.

The idea that McGill could be anyone filtered through Evan's mind. That possibility put a whole new slant on the situation.

"Get out of the boat, Hunter," Rowen ordered. She looked madder than hell.

"Let's not bother with idle chitchat," he suggested. "Come aboard and we'll be on our way."

She blinked, hesitated a moment. She hadn't expected him to surrender so easily.

Slowly she lowered the weapon. "You try anything funny and I *will* shoot you," she warned and, judging by the look in her eyes, she meant it.

Evan held up both hands. "You have my word. I won't try anything funny."

When Rowen and her partner had boarded, Evan started the engine and eased out of the slip.

Her partner took a seat, but Rowen was too fired up to relax to that degree. Instead, she moved up close to Evan at the helm.

"You're a real bastard," she snapped. "I should have known you were up to something."

He flinched at the harsh sound of her voice. She was too angry to care what he felt.

"It's true my goal was to distract you so that I could

get away," he admitted. Why lie? She wasn't that naive. "But I didn't plan what happened."

Yes, he'd planned to seduce her, talk her into a long hot bath. Except things went too far.

"Well, I hope it was worth it," she said hotly, "because any feelings I still had for you are definitely dead now."

Nothing he hadn't expected. Still, the words stabbed deep inside him.

As much as it would hurt both of them, he had to finish this once and for all now. "That's good," he said as he maneuvered through the dark water. "I wouldn't want you to harbor any false hope."

He didn't have to look at her. He felt the way his words crushed her…shuddered beneath the jarring impact to her heart.

She turned away from him, stared out over the water. But she said nothing. No matter. He felt the tide of tension gaining momentum. His own eyes burned, but he clenched his jaw against the weakness. Better for her to hate him than for her to hope.

He'd planned to do this alone but if he'd left her on that wharf, she would have followed, increasing the risk that one or both of them would be spotted.

"We'll approach from the Intertidal Zone, well away from the pier," he told her. She didn't comment.

They had both studied the map and his plan was the best way, though certainly not the easiest. Climbing those steep slopes to access the island would prove less than pleasant, but the element of surprise was the only real ammunition they possessed. He didn't want to lose it.

A streak of lightning abruptly lit up the sky. Evan blinked. Even his dark glasses weren't sufficient protection from nature's brilliant display.

"Looks like it might start raining again," Merv commented, obviously feeling left out.

"Just our luck," Rowen said.

Evan didn't join the conversation. He needed to concentrate and conserve his energy.

He switched off the engine as they neared their destination. The island looked dark. The high drumlin gave it the look of a fortress.

The tide ushered them closer to the steep bank on the side of the island opposite the pier. Once Evan was satisfied with the position, he dropped anchor.

They had no choice but to swim the rest of the way. Getting any closer would risk damaging the boat, which was their only means of escape, assuming they survived.

Evan shrugged off his coat, checked his shoulder holster and shed his gloves. He took a deep breath and braced for the impact of overpowering sensations.

Rowen watched as Hunter prepared for leaving the relative safety of the boat. As furious as she was, she recognized how damned hard this was going to be for him. And part of her, stupidly, wished she could protect him from the pain.

"Idiot," she muttered. He'd broken her heart, then

come back and stepped on it one last time after she'd finally gotten past bleeding for him every damn time she closed her eyes.

Focus. This was where things got dicey.

"Merv, you stay here and call for backup when I give you the signal or in the event you hear gunfire break out."

He shook his head and let go a heavy breath. "I'd feel a lot better, Ro, if you let me go and you stayed here."

Just what she needed. Another overprotective male. But she knew Merv. He had her best interests at heart. They'd worked together for years and could practically read each other's minds. It had nothing to do with psychic phenomena.

"Someone needs to stay behind to call for backup," she repeated. Coming here was dumb as hell without backup as it was. But she understood the reasoning. There was no way to know who they could trust. Hunter had said this guy McGill could be posing as anyone. He'd apparently given himself a new ID after disappearing just over four years ago. First order of business was confirming what was here…and what wasn't. "You know the deal," she said to Merv. She didn't have to wonder if he would understand what she meant.

"I could get Doherty over here," Merv offered nonchalantly. "He's sitting on ready."

Hunter pivoted toward her partner. "You told Doherty about this operation?"

Merv and Rowen exchanged glances; he let her explain. "We're a team, Hunter," she said flatly. "Obviously something you know nothing about. Doherty is standing by in case we need him." That's all he needed to know at this point. Hunter wasn't the only one who could keep secrets.

"He's got his finger on speed dial to the chief," Merv added smugly, miffed that Hunter would question his and Rowen's tactics.

Hunter settled his gaze on her then, though his eyes were shielded by those infuriating dark glasses. "I hope you realize the risk you've taken."

Rowen peeled off her own jacket, then shoved the extra clip for her weapon into her jeans pocket. "Screw you, Hunter. This is my case."

With that clarified, she draped her legs over the side of the boat and slipped into the cold water.

Her breath rushed out of her lungs and she gasped to reclaim it. Damn! She'd known the water would be chilly, but this was really cold.

Glutton for punishment that she was, she wondered how Hunter would deal with the sharp drop in his body temperature.

He didn't give her time to ponder the question. He slid into the water as noiselessly as an Olympic diver and started strong, steady breaststrokes toward the island.

Rowen did the same. The pull of the tide made the going easy. She'd no sooner reached the rocky slope than rain started to fall once more. Another flash of lightning lit up the sky.

Using jutting rocks for handholds and ledges for her

boots, she climbed the steep slope. The rain blurred her vision, made going slippery as hell. By the time she flung her body onto more level ground, she was breathing hard. Hunter had waited to see that she made it and then he headed for the copse of trees. Rowen scrubbed the rain from her face and followed.

Shrubs and trees provided adequate cover as they moved through the darkness. Images and sounds kept flitting through her mind. Pirates burying their treasure…sword fights…dead rabbits. She shuddered.

The lightning slashed sharply above the Boston skyline, thunder shattered the silence. She watched for Hunter's reaction, hoped he was handling this all right.

The moon did little to cut through the thick darkness. The rain had let up enough to allow the fog to rise and swirl around them as they moved toward the ruins of the old Maritime Training School.

Rowen stopped to peer toward the meadow that lay in the distance beyond the trees. Stunned, she blinked and looked again. A brand-new structure, massive in size, loomed where historic ruins had once stood. Water rippled and foamed on the beach beyond it.

The granite building resembled a fortress or an uninspired castle. The way the fog lifted around it made Rowen shudder inside. A giant mausoleum, she decided. That's what it looked like, looming in the darkness.

"So much for being closed due to contamination," Hunter murmured.

She almost jumped…hadn't realized he was that

close. She swallowed the lump of fear that had lodged in her throat. The place was contaminated all right, contaminated with whatever McGill was up to.

"Getting inside isn't going to be easy," she said, tossing out the deduction that had just crossed her mind.

"Just remember, we're only here to check it out," Hunter warned. "Taking down McGill or whoever the hell is in there is the Bureau's job."

"Yeah, yeah." He'd told her that about four times already.

"Get down!"

Rowen turned around just in time to see Hunter go hand to hand with another dark figure.

She reached for her gun.

"I wouldn't do that if I were you."

The muzzle of a weapon bored into the back of her skull.

Rowen froze.

She knew that voice.

Chapter Thirteen

"It's really quite simple."

Rowen stared, a mixture of fury and hatred churning in her gut, at Chief Bart Koppel. The son of a bitch was the one. Nathan McGill, aka the South End Murderer.

"I needed to kill four birds with one stone, so to speak," he explained.

Rowen risked a glance toward the corner of the cell where she and Hunter had been tossed. He lay on the cold stone floor. He wasn't moving. Worry twisted in her gut.

Her gaze whipped back to Koppel. "I'm going to kill you. You know that, don't you?" She said the words with all the rage and disgust mounting inside her.

If it was the last thing she did, this bastard was going down.

"Amuse yourself if you wish, Detective O'Connor," Koppel said. "Your body won't ever be found." He jerked his head toward Hunter. "Nor will his."

"Why the hell did you start this?" She shivered. Her

clothes were still wet from the swim she'd taken. The punches she'd suffered for taking a dive at Koppel had left her with a busted lip and a bloody nose. Not that she could feel any pain right now. She was too pissed off.

"Azariel had figured out I was here," Koppel explained nonchalantly. "I couldn't very well risk him deciding to do the right thing or, worse, attempting blackmail. I've worked too hard to get this operation where it is today."

What the hell was he talking about? "What are you doing here, ch—?" She bit back the title she'd respected for four years. How could this be the man she'd looked up to?

"I have clients, O'Connor." He smiled, amused by his own ingenuity. "Clients who are willing to pay any price for entertainment. *Special* entertainment. Think about it. Wouldn't it be wonderful to have your own personal psychic to let you know when to just stay home to avoid a bad day at the office?" He laughed. "Imagine what a party favorite a mind-reader could be?"

"You're sick," she hissed, disgust coiling in her stomach. "These aren't animals you're talking about!"

"Money can buy most anything these days, O'Connor, and the Internet makes international sales a snap. I just cornered the market on a new trend, that's all." He waved his arms magnanimously. "I built this place as a sort of waiting station and, of course, as a test facility. When my team finds what I'm looking for, this is where the package is delivered for testing and verification before final delivery to the customer with the winning bid. There's no place on earth like it."

He was crazy. The manic look in his eyes confirmed her conclusion. "So all of it—six innocent victims—was about setting up Viktor to get him off your back?"

"Come now, Detective, do I look that shallow?" he scoffed. "No, no. I not only needed to get Viktor off my scent, I needed to get rid of Jeff. He was the last of my blood…the only person who might have inadvertently recognized some of my old habits."

He shrugged and let go a heavy breath. "Unfortunately I had to extend that umbrella to include you, as well. The Homicide unit won't be the same without you. You're a fine detective, perhaps too good. I had begun to see that I wouldn't be able to pull this off without alerting you." Koppel glanced at Hunter. "And, of course, your protector. If anything happened to you he wouldn't rest until he got his vengeance. Might as well get rid of him in the process. Azariel, of course, will be blamed for all the murders. Using the drug his company manufacturers was the clincher. Case closed. Thanks for your outstanding detective work."

Rowen shook her head. This was too crazy. "But you've been my chief since I came on board at Homicide. Five years ago, McGill worked for the Bureau." Maybe the chief had developed some sort of bizarre mental disorder. Maybe he'd lost his mind. God, she was grasping at straws here.

Another of those smug smiles slid across his face. "I had to pick a life. Making one up isn't nearly as much fun or as reliable. Plus I needed a position that would keep me in the know. What better one than this? Once Koppel's wife was out of the way, it was easy to take over. He had no children or other family. No friends to speak of. I monitored his activities long enough to feel comfortable with the transition and then, *voilà*." He indicated his face. "A little necessary cosmetic surgery and I became him."

Something he'd said filtered through the haze of disbelief. "Did you cause the accident that killed the chief's wife?" Surely that couldn't be.

He snickered. "How else could I get rid of a perfectly healthy woman?"

She'd heard enough. "You might as well kill me, you son of a bitch, because if I live through this I'm taking you down." She fisted her hands and challenged him to make a move.

"Let's not be so dramatic, O'Connor." He moved toward her one step, then a second one. "I'm going to use you and your lover here to drive the final nail in Azariel's coffin."

Fear trickled through her. "I'll kill myself before I'll let you use me for anything!"

Koppel or McGill, whoever the hell he was, pulled a syringe from his jacket. "We can't let that happen, now can we?"

Rowen glanced around the stark cell. There was nothing to grab for a weapon.

"You'll only feel a slight pinprick and then nothing at all," he cajoled as he moved closer. "Paralysis will be instantaneous, but this dosage isn't lethal. It'll just keep you out of my way for a while...until I've gotten Azariel into place."

"Backup will be here any minute now," she threatened, her heart pumping wildly as he came ever nearer.

"You mean the backup your partner was supposed to call?" He shook his head. "I don't think he even heard my men coming. It's hell when a man gets old. Merv should have retired years ago."

Rowen slammed a punch into his gut. He grunted but still managed to grab her by the hair.

She twisted away from the needle, elbowed him in the side. She kicked his shins, roared with the force of it. She wanted to kill him.

He screamed obscenities at her. Snapped her head back, exposing her neck as that damned needle came closer and closer.

The hand holding the syringe suddenly was jerked away from her.

Koppel screamed and his hold on her hair relaxed.

She spun around just in time to see Hunter empty the syringe into Koppel's neck.

A look of horror claimed his face and he went limp.

Hunter let him drop to the floor.

"Grab his key card," he ordered.

Her movements frantic, matching her racing pulse, she quickly dug through his pockets until she found the key card he'd used to access the locked doors around this place.

"I thought you were dead," she mentioned offhandedly.

"I've heard that before."

Her gaze collided with Hunter's. "Are you all right?"

From the sound of his voice, he definitely was not all right. The left side of his face had begun to swell from the beating he'd taken, and his voice wavered when he spoke.

"I'll live. Now let's get out of here."

"Wait." Rowen stood, shoved the hair out of her face. Unlike Hunter, she'd been conscious when they dragged her into this cell. "In some places, access requires his thumbprint."

Hunter swore.

Just then, Rowen would have given most anything for a good sharp knife, but she didn't have one handy.

Before she could fathom his intent, Hunter knelt down and slung Koppel over his shoulder.

"Let's go."

To exit the cell, she needed only the key card. When the door opened, she surveyed the corridor to make sure no guards were around. But there could be cameras.

"They're probably watching us," she warned, her breath ragged with the adrenaline pumping through her veins.

"Probably," he agreed, his voice strained from lugging the chief's deadweight. "Listen to me, *Rowen*."

She looked up at him, the pain in his eyes almost undoing her. "Yeah?"

"There's no way I'm getting out of here." He held up a hand when she was about to interrupt. "I'm too weak.

But I'm going to try and get you out of here. Go for help. Call. Swim. Do whatever you have to."

"Just hang on, Hunter," she urged. "I wasn't kidding when I told Koppel backup was on the way. Merv and I have this system. When I told him to stay behind so he could call backup, that's exactly what he did. Five minutes after we left him."

"What if they got to him first?"

That was entirely possible. "We'll just have to pray they didn't."

A beat of silence passed.

"Let's go."

Taking a deep breath, Rowen moved out into the corridor. She hurried toward the entrance she'd been hustled through. This one required the key card and Koppel's thumbprint. She slid the card and then twisted his hand into a position where she could flatten his thumb as needed. The door opened.

She eased through the opening, checked left, then right.

The business end of a Beretta met her.

"I'm looking for the exit," she said with a big, feigned smile.

The guard jerked her into the corridor. "Where's your escort?"

Before she could answer the guy crumpled to the floor.

She shrugged. "Obviously he didn't know there were two of us."

"Get his weapon."

"You read my mind." She grabbed the Beretta. "What about him?"

"Drag him through that door and take his key card."

It wasn't easy, but Rowen did as instructed. "This way," she said when she hurried around Hunter to lead once more.

The door at the other end of the corridor started to open. Hunter pushed her toward the closest side door. Her hand shaking, she passed the key card through the slide and shoved the door inward. No sooner had it closed than she heard the sound of boots pounding in the corridor.

She let go a shaky breath.

Close. Too close.

"Don't turn on the light," Hunter warned.

She couldn't be sure if it was for his comfort or to avoid attracting attention.

He plopped Koppel onto a desk and walked over to what looked like windows draped with blinds. He parted two slats and peered beyond the window.

When he drew back, he turned to her. It was too dark to see his eyes, but his voice said it all. "Take a look at this."

She joined him by the window and peeked through the blinds. Shock radiated through her.

This was no window, this was a viewing center. What looked like cases lined the walls of the room below. People—she gasped—slept on narrow cots behind those steel bars. In the center of the room were computers and examination tables. The lab for confirming what his prisoners were capable of. A human zoo.

"God only knows how many he's done this to," she murmured. "Koppel said he'd been selling them."

"I heard." Hunter took a rough breath, amping up her concern.

"I thought you were…"

"I was just playing dead."

She was glad. He'd saved her life and his own, as well.

"He had the perfect setup," Hunter said, his attention turning back to the business below. "No one would be nosing around on this island. He could do anything he wanted."

Until Viktor found him out.

"I'm going to search for a phone," she told Hunter. They had to get the hell out of here. There would be more guards. An operation like this would have tight security and she couldn't be certain Merv made that call before…she couldn't think about her partner right now. And she had to help these people.

Before she could put the concept into action, an alarm sounded. The people downstairs began to scurry about to protect their prisoners. There were more hurried footsteps in the corridor.

Hunter hefted Koppel back onto his shoulder.

"I guess this means he killed the real chief," she said absently. She'd only just thought of that. Her chest constricted. How could she not have noticed?

"That would be my guess," Hunter said wearily.

Rowen stalled at the door. "How can we ever be sure of anyone?" It seemed incredible that taking over a life so completely was actually possible.

His hand touched her cheek. "There are ways."

He was right about that. The eyes could be fooled…even the ears could be duped. But when a man and woman made love, that was a dance that couldn't be faked. But McGill had gotten around that by killing the chief's wife.

Rowen ordered her attention back to the task at hand—getting the hell out of there. She could grieve her chief and her partner later after she'd brought down the people behind their murders.

They moved through the next two doors without incident. Rowen recognized the area. They were almost out of this damned nightmare. Wherever the hell all the security personnel had headed, it was definitely not this way. Maybe fate was on Rowen's side tonight.

"This way," she said over her shoulder.

Hunter nodded, but then he fell to his knees.

She rushed back to him, tried to help him up.

"Go," he growled. "I'm finished."

She shoved Koppel off him.

"You have to make it." She grabbed Hunter by the arm and tried to haul him to his feet.

He groaned savagely. "Just go."

She crouched down in front of him, made him look at her. His eyes were bloodshot as if he'd been on a week-long drinking binge, and his skin looked as pale as a ghost.

"Why can't you walk? Are you hurt?"

Stupid questions, she knew. But she had to ascertain some kind of status on his condition.

"It's the medication," he managed to say brokenly. "I had to take an extra dose…too much."

Hell. She didn't know what to do about that. "Just try," she urged. "Try to stand and then you can lean on me."

She got back to her feet and tugged. She managed to get him to his feet. When he leaned on her, she almost went down, but she locked her knees and didn't give in.

"Come on. We can make it." She shoved the next door open.

She considered how the wailing alarm sirens were surely affecting him. She looked upward. The glaring fluorescent lights. God, he must be in horrific pain. She had to get him out of here. Into the darkness…away from the sound.

One more door. Just another fifty yards.

She walked as fast as she could with his weight bearing down on her.

Almost there.

She braced against the door as she slid the key card. The lock released and then she pushed it open. The cool air hit her in the face and she thanked God for it.

Floodlights weaved around the property, but she ignored them. The sound of a bullhorn stopped her half-way to the copse of trees they'd used as cover earlier.

"Boston police. Drop your weapons… Surrender."

Relief hurtled through her. Backup was here.

Hot damn! Merv had come through for her.

"Halt!"

Rowen twisted her head around to see who'd shouted at them. "Boston PD!" she shouted back, identifying herself in the event it was another cop.

"Don't move!"

She turned her head a little farther, and adrenaline flared in her chest. It was one of Koppel's security team.

"Drop your weapon," she demanded. "Don't you hear that?" She cocked her head and listened to the orders being repeated for all to hear. "It's over."

"I have my orders," he said grimly as he took aim. "You aren't to leave this island alive."

"No!"

She tried to shove Hunter to the ground, but she couldn't move quickly enough. His body jerked with the impact of the bullet. Fear knocked the breath out of her.

When she was about to run headlong into the shooter to take him down, a bullet whizzed past her right ear.

She dropped to the ground.

"Take that, you bastard!" Another shot exploded in the air.

Rowen looked up to see her partner stalking toward

the downed security guard, another round ensuring the guy wouldn't be getting back up.

"I thought they killed you…" Her voice trailed off.

Her mind whirled with too many questions…too much insanity. Her head started to spin, blackness threatened. Can't pass out, she ordered.

"They tried." Merv stuffed his weapon back into its holster, sauntered over to her and offered his hand. "All I had to do was sink like a rock as soon as I hit the water. Damn fools thought they'd got me."

He hoisted her to her feet.

Hunter.

Fear seized her again. She rushed to him, dropped to her knees. He lay deathly still.

"We need help," she cried out, her gaze desperately seeking her partner's. "Fast!"

Merv was on the horn already. She heard the words he shouted into his cell phone, knowing those instructions would be passed along to any medical personnel involved in the invasion of Boston PD all around them.

"No heartbeat," she told Merv, her voice trembling. Her icy hands shaking as badly as her voice, she ripped open Hunter's shirt. Blood poured from a wound almost dead center of his chest.

"I got the wound. Give him some air, Ro!"

Merv was on his knees, too. He'd flattened his palm over the wound to staunch the flood of blood.

Instinct took over, and Rowen performed the steps

she'd been trained to do a dozen times over. Check the airway…quick breaths…chest compressions…

"Hang on, pal," Merv muttered.

Suddenly someone else was there, taking over, pushing Rowen aside—paramedics.

She stumbled back out of the way…tears blurring her vision.

Hunter hadn't moved.

He looked so pale.

Merv took her into his arms. "Don't watch, Ro. It's bad. It's real bad."

She pulled free of his hold. "I have to see," she growled savagely. Then she remembered Koppel. She grabbed her partner by the lapels. "It's Koppel," she explained. "He's the one who started this…we left him in a room…." She shook her head. "Somewhere, I don't know where. He got a shot of his own medicine. He's paralyzed, but he'll come out of it anytime now. Don't let him get away."

Merv nodded and bounded off to find that bastard Koppel, though he had no idea why their chief would be a part of this. Rowen would explain everything to him later.

"We're losing him!"

Her attention swung back to where Hunter lay on the ground. The two paramedics were working frantically to get his heart beating once more.

Please, God, she prayed. *Don't let him die.*

"Clear!"

She had to turn away as they attempted to shock his heart back into a rhythm.

The whop-whop-whop of a helicopter's blades cut through the air. She wanted to be glad for speedy transport, but she couldn't think just now. Hunter was dying right before her eyes, and there was nothing she could do to stop it.

Someone was suddenly ushering her away.

She looked up to see a Boston policeman on either side of her. "We'll take you to the hospital, ma'am," one of them explained.

What?

She looked back to Hunter, but he wasn't on the ground anymore. He was being loaded into the helicopter. "I want to go with—"

"There's no room, Detective O'Connor. We'll get you there as fast as possible."

She looked back one last time, watched the helicopter lift off the ground.

Hunter was dead. She didn't have to be told. She could feel it.

He was dead.

Chapter Fourteen

Dr. Bruce McBee glanced at the readout on the cardiac monitor—the pattern of a heart struggling to stay ahead of the Grim Reaper.

Tension zipped through the surgeon who had been in this very position many times before. A patient's survival depended upon three things—the skill of the surgeon and his team, time and plain old luck.

The patient had lost a massive amount of blood. An IV of Ringer's solution, as well as fresh O-positive blood, was running wide-open into his veins and still he barely hung on.

Evan Hunter had been wheeled into a trauma room, stripped naked, intubated and slapped on a ventilator…no time for an operating room or fancy preparations.

He'd coded twice en route.

"BP's dropping, Doctor."

Anticipation only sharpening his precise movements, Dr. McBee glanced at the nurse, then back to the hemostats that had kept the patient from completely exsanguinating. The bullet had nipped the atrium, the wall of the heart. At this point, blood no longer pooled in the thoracic cavity, but the damage had already been done. Vitals were unstable. The patient was weak and losing ground with each passing second. With the bullet removed, all Dr. McBee could do was repair the damage and hope this man was strong enough to bounce back from the sustained trauma.

His life hung in the balance despite the best surgical team Boston Mass. had to offer.

Carefully, McBee stitched together the edges of the puncture. As swiftly and deftly as humanly possible, he repaired and checked the damage, then closed the necessary incision he'd performed himself in opening up the patient's damaged chest.

"Losing his pressure!"

McBee frowned. "Don't die now, Mr. Hunter," he murmured. "We've got you patched up."

"V tach!"

Ventricular tachycardia was a potentially lethal disruption of the normal heartbeat. In this patient's case, definitely lethal. He was already immensely weak from significant blood loss and shock from serious physical trauma.

"Start CPR," McBee ordered.

The organized chaos built to a crescendo as the entire team worked to save the patient's life. The nurse, her hands on the patient's sternum, was pumping his chest, cardiac compressions that would send life-giving blood to the brain.

No response.

"Shock him."

McBee glanced at the monitor.

Nothing.

"Again."

Sweat formed on the surgeon's forehead. He and his team struggled for many minutes to regain a heart rhythm, but their efforts proved futile. McBee hated to get this close to success only to fail due to human frailty.

Finally, he relented. He stepped back. "Call it."

His team looked at him, then at each other before stepping back, as well, leaving Evan Hunter to rest in peace on the table.

A moment of silence passed. No one liked to admit defeat.

One of the nurses announced the time of death, making the call official.

It was over.

ROWEN SAT in the E.R. lobby. Stared vacantly. Merv had come to sit with her. Had offered her coffee. Cola. Anything to get her to do something besides just sit there. But she couldn't. She just couldn't. She kept seeing Hunter lying there, unresponsive to the paramedics' efforts.

He'd known he would die when he came here.

She didn't know how she knew that, but she did. Maybe he'd told her.

She should have told him that she forgave him for walking out on her before. Now it was too late. She'd never get to explain that she had still loved him anyway.

"I have to…" She hurried out of the room, walked down the deathly quiet corridor until she found the nearest ladies' room.

She grabbed the basin for support and let her emotions get the better of her. She cried. Cried so hard her entire body shook with the violence of it.

It just wasn't fair….

Hadn't he suffered enough?

After a few more minutes, she pulled herself back together. She should get back out there…wanted to be there when the doctor came with news. She bent over the sink and washed her face with cool water. Her fingers shook and she tried hard to scrape up some control, but the effort was just too much.

Her heart felt like a rock in her chest.

She straightened, reached for a paper towel.

She jerked, lost her breath. Her reflection was not the only one in the mirror.

Viktor Azariel stood behind her.

She wheeled around. "What do you want?"

A new wave of agony washed over her, forcing the tears cresting on her lashes to fall. She didn't ever want to see anyone or anything related to this case again.

He reached out, swiped a hot tear from her cheek before she could dodge his touch. "Why the tears, Detective O'Connor?"

She had to clamp down on her lower lip to keep from howling in pain. What the hell was wrong with this bastard? Didn't he know what was tearing her apart? He'd sure as hell appeared to read her mind before.

"Get out," she said when she'd found enough control. "I don't want you here. You were wrong—it wasn't me who was next…it was Hunter."

She couldn't meet his eyes any longer. Just looking at him made her shudder in agony. Why didn't he go away?

He shook his head, making those long silky strands of dark hair sway back and forth in a mesmerizing fashion against the backdrop of his white shirt.

"You must have more faith, *Rowen*," he said, mimicking the way Hunter said her name.

A sob burst from her lips. How could he taunt her like this? "Bastard," she choked out.

He reached for her hand, held on when she tried to jerk it away, then flattened her palm against his chest…over his heart. "Feel that," he said in that voice that had the power to make her pay attention when all she wanted to do was die.

Somehow, she nodded.

"His heart beats for you…."

She jerked her hand away and covered her face. She didn't want to hear any more…

"He's like me," Viktor whispered. "No mere bullet can kill him. Again he took your place and will live to tell about it."

Rowen scrubbed at the new flood of tears and opened

her eyes so that she could see Viktor's face when she told him what she thought of him.

He was gone.

She blinked, struggled to catch her breath.

Maybe she'd imagined him.

The door suddenly opened. "Ro! The doctor's looking for you."

The next few minutes were one big blur for Rowen. Dr. McBee, the surgeon, kept repeating himself.

We thought we'd lost him, but somehow he survived. His heart just started beating again.

The only thing that mattered to Rowen was the fact that Hunter was still alive.

And Viktor had dropped by to tell her.

HE CRACKED his eyes open slowly, uncertain what he would find.

Evan wondered if he was dead or alive.

He vaguely remembered someone calling his time of death.

Had he dreamed that?

He also recalled seeing Viktor somewhere amid the chaos. Probably a dream, as well.

Where was Rowen?

He needed to know that she was all right.

Using all his might, he forced his eyes open.

Bright lights.

He squeezed them shut again, waited for the shock of pain that would follow the exposure to the lights.

Seconds, or maybe minutes, passed and no pain.

Curious now, he opened his eyes again and gave himself time to focus.

White room. Beeping sounds.

He turned his head to the right. A barrage of monitors tracked his vitals.

Hospital.

He looked down. A white sheet covered him from the waist down. A bandage had been plastered across his chest.

Gut shot.

He remembered now and slowly became aware of the pain shimmering just beneath the barrier the painkillers provided. In all likelihood, he should be dead just now.

Rowen.

He turned his head to the left and his breath stilled in his lungs.

She was curled up in a chair next to his bed. His heart picked up an extra beat. She looked rumpled and a little scratched up, but basically unharmed.

He tried to say her name, but his mouth was too dry. He moistened his lips, struggled to clear his throat, then made a second effort.

"*Rowen,*" came out, rusty and croaky. His arms felt too heavy to lift, preventing him from reaching for her.

Her eyes flew open and she was at his bedside before he could say more.

"You're awake."

Her voice sounded…normal. Didn't cause him any discomfort.

With monumental effort, he moved his left hand over the sheet, scarcely heard the rasp of sound. How was that possible? He didn't understand.

He spotted the IVs then. Drugs, the painkillers. Powerful ones, no doubt.

But then he remembered that painkillers wouldn't do the trick, had never provided him any relief. Every kind known to man had been tried on him three years ago.

"What happened to me?" he asked, trying to clear his throat.

The sound of his own voice startled him. The vibrations against his eardrums were tolerable...normal, like it used to be. Hope surged through his veins, but he beat it back. He couldn't endure the disappointment if this relief proved to be short-lived.

"You were shot." She looked away, as if what she needed to say next was more than she could bear to impart. "It was bad, Hunter. The surgeon said he thought he lost you. Your heart stopped for two full minutes."

The only escape outside the healing is death.

Viktor's words echoed in his brain.

Evan had technically been dead for two whole minutes.

"It's a miracle you're alive. You lost so much blood." She sighed, swiped at her suspiciously bright eyes. "But you're fine now." She managed a sad smile. "The doctor says you'll fully recover. He couldn't believe it. He said it was as if everything shut down, then two minutes later rebooted."

Her eyes closed and she shook her head, her lips

trembling. "I was so afraid I'd lost you." She opened her eyes then and looked directly into his. "I don't know why you walked away and never came back three years ago, but it doesn't matter. I loved you then, I love you now. If you go away again, I'll still love you." She took a breath. "There, I said it. If that makes me a fool, I guess I'll just have to live with it."

Evan's chest tightened and it had nothing to do with the surgery. He had to tell her. "It's gone, *Rowen*."

She looked confused at first, but then her eyes rounded in disbelief. She looked up at the lights. "They don't hurt your eyes." Not a question…she'd just made the connection.

"Not at all."

"Your hearing is…normal?"

"Yes."

"Oh, my, God!" She bent down and kissed him right on the mouth. She drew back just far enough to look into his eyes again. "I swear, Hunter, I don't care what I said a minute ago. If you leave me again, I'll kill you."

He laughed, the tenderness in his chest made him regret it. "Let me recover from this injury before you go threatening me, Detective."

She shoved her hair behind her ears, her fingers smoothing the silky strands, making him wish he could do the same. "I'm sorry. I don't know what I'm saying. This has been…" She moistened her lips, searched for the right words.

"A long, long nightmare," he finished for her.

She nodded. "Too long."

He turned his palm up and waited for her to take his hand. He didn't have the strength to reach out to her the way he wanted to, but he needed a connection. "I didn't want to drag you into hell with me," he confessed. "That's why I didn't come back. I lied to you before."

She stared at their joined hands for a time. "You know Koppel or McGill, whoever the hell he is, probably had something to do with what happened to your team—to get the last of the Gateway investigators out of the way."

"Probably."

She shrugged, exhaustion sagging her delicate shoulders. "Maybe he'll fess up to save his hide and then we'll know what really happened." A sigh whispered out of her. "I keep thinking about all those people he was keeping on that island and all the others he sold into slavery."

"Getting to the bottom of all he's done is the Bureau's job," Evan assured her. "They'll find a way to track down his client list."

Rowen nodded. She fidgeted with the sheet a moment. "Agent Braham is already on it. He stopped in to check on you a few hours ago. So getting back to us, does this confession of yours mean that since you appear to be well, there's room for an *us* in your future?"

He squeezed her hand as best he could. "If you'll have me."

"You saved my life—it's the least I can do," she

teased. And then she leaned down and brushed her lips across his. The sweet sensation trembled through him the way it was meant to. God, how he'd missed her.

"As soon as I'm out of here," he said between her soft kisses, "we'll have to make sure the rest of me is still in working order."

She smiled. "What kind of detective would I be if I didn't follow up on your case to the fullest extent possible? The investigation might even require house arrest…and I know just the place."

Listening to her voice and watching her expressions with no barriers between them and without pain was more than he could have hoped for. Fate had given him a second chance, or perhaps it was a miracle. Whatever it was, he would not waste it, not a single second.

* * * * *

Look for Debra Webb's next book,
THE COLBY CONSPIRACY,
coming in October from
Signature Select.

Victoria Colby-Camp could feel the subtle shift…the ever-so-slight change in the very atmosphere of her happy but fragile world. Evil was headed her way once more.

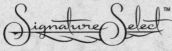

MINISERIES

National bestselling author

Debra Webb

FILES FROM THE COLBY AGENCY

Two favorite novels from her
bestselling Colby Agency series—
plus Bonus Features

Love and danger go hand in hand for two
Colby Agency operatives in these two
exciting full-length stories!

Coming in September.

**Bonus Features
include:**

**The Writing Life,
Trivia
and an exclusive
Sneak Peek!**

Where love comes alive™

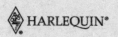

If you enjoyed what you just read,
then we've got an offer you can't resist!

Take 2 bestselling love stories FREE!

Plus get a FREE surprise gift!

Clip this page and mail it to Harlequin Reader Service®

IN U.S.A.
3010 Walden Ave.
P.O. Box 1867
Buffalo, N.Y. 14240-1867

IN CANADA
P.O. Box 609
Fort Erie, Ontario
L2A 5X3

YES! Please send me 2 free Harlequin Intrigue® novels and my free surprise gift. After receiving them, if I don't wish to receive anymore, I can return the shipping statement marked cancel. If I don't cancel, I will receive 4 brand-new novels each month, before they're available in stores! In the U.S.A., bill me at the bargain price of $4.24 plus 25¢ shipping and handling per book and applicable sales tax, if any*. In Canada, bill me at the bargain price of $4.99 plus 25¢ shipping and handling per book and applicable taxes**. That's the complete price and a savings of at least 10% off the cover prices—what a great deal! I understand that accepting the 2 free books and gift places me under no obligation ever to buy any books. I can always return a shipment and cancel at any time. Even if I never buy another book from Harlequin, the 2 free books and gift are mine to keep forever.

181 HDN DZ7N
381 HDN DZ7P

Name _____ (PLEASE PRINT) _____

Address _____ Apt.# _____

City _____ State/Prov. _____ Zip/Postal Code _____

Not valid to current Harlequin Intrigue® subscribers.

Want to try two free books from another series?
Call 1-800-873-8635 or visit www.morefreebooks.com.

* Terms and prices subject to change without notice. Sales tax applicable in N.Y.
** Canadian residents will be charged applicable provincial taxes and GST.
   All orders subject to approval. Offer limited to one per household.
   ® are registered trademarks owned and used by the trademark owner and or its licensee.

INT04R   ©2004 Harlequin Enterprises Limited

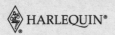